A PROPER DARCY CHRISTMAS

A Delightful
Pride and Prejudice
Christmas Romance

Pamela Aidan

Copyright © 2022 by Pamela Aidan

All rights reserved. No part of this publication may be reproduced, distributed or transmitted in any form or by any means, including photocopying, recording, or other electronic or mechanical methods, without the prior written permission of the publisher, except in the case of brief quotations embodied in critical reviews and certain other noncommercial uses permitted by copyright law. For permission requests, write to the publisher, addressed "Attention: Permissions Coordinator," at the address below.

Pamela Aidan
www.traipsingafterjane.wordpress.com

Publisher's Note: This is a work of fiction. Names, characters, places, and incidents are a product of the author's imagination. Locales and public names are sometimes used for atmospheric purposes. Any resemblance to actual people, living or dead, or to businesses, companies, events, institutions, or locales is completely coincidental.

Book Layout ©2017 BookDesignTemplates.com

Cover design ©2022 Getcovers.com
A Proper Darcy Christmas/ Pamela Aidan. -- 1st ed.
ISBN 979-8-3660872-7-8

Dedicated in loving memory of our granddaughter, Maddie. Madison May Mogen: 2001—2022

*Love suffers long and is kind;
love does not envy;
love does not parade itself
is not puffed up;
does not behave rudely,
does not seek its own,
is not provoked,
thinks no evil;
does not rejoice in iniquity,
but rejoices in the truth;
bears all things, believes all things,
hopes all things, endures all things.
Love never fails.*

−1 Corinthians 13:4-8 NJKV

Contents

Chapter 1 1
Chapter 2 15
Chapter 3 23
Chapter 4 33
Chapter 5 41
Chapter 6 49
Chapter 7 61
Chapter 8 69
Chapter 9 81
Chapter 10 91
Chapter 11 101
Chapter 12 111
Chapter 13 121
Chapter 14 131
Chapter 15 143
Chapter 16 155
Chapter 17 167
Chapter 18 177
Epilogue 185
A Christmas Carol 189
More from Pamela Aidan 190
What's Coming Next 192
About the Author 195

Chapter 1

Sunday, December 12, 1813

Snow fell gently from wind torn clouds onto the moonlit fields and forests of the great estate of Pemberley, wrapping man and beast, master and servant in a silence deeper than was usually wont to occur in mid-December. Fitzwilliam Darcy lay in a profound slumber in what had come to be designated as "his" side of the great bed that dominated the pale gold and rose bedchamber suite known as the Darcy Rooms. In that same great bed, but most assuredly on "her" side of it, lay his beloved wife. Elizabeth Darcy's slumber, however, was not as profound as her adored husband's. In fact, her young form, richly thick and aglow with new life, was beginning to stir. Impulses toward a wonderfully anticipated future were even now coursing through it, causing her to whimper lightly and throw out a hand curved beseechingly in her disturbed sleep.

At the slight noise, the hound, who lay on the carpet at the foot of the bed, raised his head. Alert now to his mistress's distress, he heaved himself to his feet and padded around to investigate. Elizabeth's outstretched hand puzzled him. Did she wish to pet him? He peered at her face, but found no further clue there. Stepping closer, he pushed his nose against her hand and then sat down and waited. No welcoming movement of her fingers ensued, but another, sharper whimper escaped her lips as she stirred uncomfortably in the bed and brought her hand back under the blankets and to her distended abdomen. Disquieted, the hound rose and trotted around to the other side of the bed and, with no pretence to delicacy, stood on his hindquarters, his front paws on the bed and thrust his cold nose into his master's face.

"Ughhh ... Trafalgar! What the devil!" Darcy screwed his face and wiped away at the wet coldness as a low rumbly noise informed him that the hound would not be gainsaid by frown or curse. Rather, Trafalgar pushed at him again, his shoulder this time, and whined. "What?" Instinctively, Darcy looked over at Elizabeth across the expanse of their bed. The past two months of her pregnancy had been physically trying and by mutual consent, a bit of distance had been agreed upon for the comfort of both. His eyes met hers, now wide, darkly glazed pools in a face gone unnaturally pale.

"Fitzwilliam," she gasped and reached out to him.

"Is it time? The baby ... ?" He took her hand in a gesture of comfort, but already she was preoccupied, her eyes closed now and her lips pressed into a thin line against the pangs gripping her body. Fear and excitement and love...and fear played havoc with his senses until a breathy sigh of pain set him into motion. He rolled out of their bed, and pulling on a robe, strode quickly through Elizabeth's dressing room and to her maid's door.

"Ellen...Ellen!" he called as he rapped on the door. In moments it cracked open and a young serving girl peered out at him. "Ellen, go fetch Mrs. Darcy's maid! Then rouse Mrs. Roseby ... and then Mrs. Reynolds. Quickly, girl!"

Almost exactly a year and a month had passed since the glorious day that marked the marriage of Pemberley's master to his dearest, loveliest Elizabeth. The time had not been one of bliss upon bliss. How could it be otherwise with such naturally strong-willed lovers? Often a humbling on both of their parts was required as they learned to be husband and wife together. Each lesson, though hard at first, proved again the satisfaction Darcy had discovered in pleasing a woman worthy of being pleased. Now the next step in their marriage was upon them with all the uncertainty and fear attendant upon a joyous hope for the future.

He turned away from the door, intent upon returning to his wife, but a sudden tremor of cold apprehension shook him while the quiet darkness of Elizabeth's dressing room gave way to the loud and rapid beating of his heart. Darcy took a deep breath and then slowly let it escape him in an attempt to calm himself. It was all so new, so fraught with dangers! What if...? He had kept that question at bay for the majority of the past nine months, pushing it off as unprofitable speculation whenever it threatened to possess him. Now it was here. The next hours would answer all *what ifs* as either useless fears or dread realities. Darcy threw back his shoulders. Whatever came, Elizabeth needed his confidence, not his fears. She would have it!

He returned to the bedside, and leaning over her, kissed Elizabeth's forehead and took her hand. "The mid-wife and Mrs. Fletcher will be here in moments." His eyes searched her face which had now relaxed somewhat but was still unnaturally pale. "How do you feel, my love?"

"All is quiet at the moment." She managed a small smile and brought his hand to her lips. A whine rose from the bedside and a pair of velvety ears and deep brown eyes appeared, followed by a moist black nose. The dog whined again and pawed at the bedclothes. Elizabeth laughed softly. "I think Trafalgar needs reassurance, my dear...perhaps more than I."

"Perhaps." Darcy cocked a sceptical eye at his hound. "Or he merely wants to regain the centre of attention. Down, Monster!" he commanded. Trafalgar humphed his disappointment but slid from the bedside and curled up where he could best view the drama that was developing.

"What time is it?" Elizabeth asked, her breath catching.

Darcy glanced at the clock on the mantle. The sight of the banked embers roused him. "Almost three o'clock. Should you like the fire stirred up?"

"I do not know ... I cannot think." She closed her eyes. "How silly of me!"

"Hush," he whispered, kissing her forehead again. "We shall wait for Mrs. Roseby's direction. I am told that she is very particular." A sharp rap sounded on the door.

"Mrs. Darcy," Annie Fletcher's voice came through from the hall, "May we come in, Ma'am?"

Upon Darcy's quick affirmation, the door opened smartly to reveal the mid-wife, Mrs. Roseby. Her air of command was unmistakable, displaying not the least concern that her call had come in the very early hours of morning. She curtsied briefly and approached the bedside. Behind her, Annie Fletcher did the same, while Ellen ventured hesitantly no further than inside the door, the eyes in her thin, young face like saucers.

Darcy stepped away for the two older women and then rounded the bed, the better to observe what was happening. The mid-wife's calm yet keen countenance quieted the agitation that had begun to appear again in Elizabeth's eyes. It did no less for his own.

"How many pains have you had, Mistress?" Mrs. Roseby asked as she felt Elizabeth's forehead and then searched for her pulse.

"Three," Elizabeth replied, "I think."

"And how far apart were they, Ma'am?"

"I ... I do not know!" Elizabeth looked at her husband in panic. He started to lean across the bed, but Mrs. Roseby forestalled him with an outstretched hand.

"There, there," she crooned. "Tis to be expected. Now that we are here, we will keep watch for you. Mr. Darcy, sir." She straightened as she addressed him. "Mrs.

Reynolds is preparing a repast that will be served in the library. We will summon you when there is news."

Darcy looked up at her in surprise and some displeasure. Evidently, he was dismissed.

~~&~~

Darcy and Trafalgar kept to the library for the greater part of the day, breaking their vigil briefly with a few steps out of doors for some air and exercise. The new snow delighted the hound for some minutes, but his shorthaired coat was no adequate protection against the cold, and after a few snowballs and a skid across the cobbled stable yard, he was content to return to the library fire. A note now lay on the desk, a response from the Bingleys to his dash that Elizabeth was in labour and that they were welcome to come at any hour.

"We will arrive tomorrow as soon as may be," Bingley wrote, "for Jane is mad to see her sister. I shall bring something special to toast the occasion. Bear up, my friend!"

Tossing the note into the grate, Darcy tarried to warm up by the flames. Charles and Jane had only recently moved to their newly purchased estate in Derbyshire and were still setting their house in order. Fortunate indeed, they had moved before the snow set in, but snow or not, his friend had vowed to make the move away from Hertfordshire—and Mrs. Bennet, their mother-in-law—no matter the weather. Darcy was entirely in sympathy, although he would not say so in front of his dear wife, and welcomed his friend and sister-in-law into the county and their country circle with pleasure. It would be a fine thing to have them here tomorrow in the face of the changes that were coming.

He had made a show at eating lunch and then, to his consternation, fell asleep on the library settee soon after. Awaking with a start, he rose, and by way of contrition, crept up to their bedchamber door for news, only to be shooed away by Annie Fletcher, Elizabeth's lady's maid, who then quickly turned back to the cry that came from behind her and shut the door. Trafalgar scratched at it to no avail and then cocked an ear at his master as if in question of his next move.

"Back to the library, I suppose," he told the hound, looking worriedly at the door. Demanding entrance would be unseemly, and to what end? He could do little to help and Elizabeth was likely beyond his comfort. He would merely be in the way and helpless, a feeling he neither relished nor a condition he wished her to see. With Trafalgar trailing behind him, he walked back to the library and, sighing, drew out papers from a case that Hinchcliffe had sent up from London which he had been neglecting and settled once more upon the settee. "You know you are not to be on the furniture," he addressed his hound while the animal finished curling up next to him. Trafalgar only snorted and laid his head on his master's lap. "Yes, well, do not let Elizabeth find you out." At the mention of her name, Darcy's thoughts returned to the barred room and the sound that had called Annie Fletcher back to her mistress's side. His heart clenched, and for a time, Heaven's mercy was beseeched.

Less than an hour later, Darcy looked up to the sound of both Mr. and Mrs. Reynolds entering the room. Might they have a word with him? There was some irregularity in the kitchen stores for which his opinion was required. Would he come and settle the matter?

"Kitchen stores?" Darcy looked at her with surprise. Never in his life had he been called upon for anything that had to do with the cook's realm.

"Yes, sir," affirmed Reynolds. He glanced behind him and then, with an odd look on his face, offered an explanation. "Mrs. Darcy would have seen to it, but ... well—"

Darcy set aside his papers and rose. "Of course. If it is urgent, Mrs. Darcy cannot be taxed with it at present."

They were at the bottom of the stairs to the kitchen hall when Darcy heard the sound of running footsteps behind them and Ellen's voice calling out, "The master, where is the master?" Racing back up the stairs, he met the girl in the doorway. "Oh, Mr. Darcy!" Recovering herself, Ellen dropped a curtsey and delivered her rehearsed message. "Mrs. Roseby sends her compliments, sir, on the birth of a fine, healthy boy and allows that if you will come no sooner than a half hour, Mrs. Darcy will be ready to receive you."

"All is well?" Darcy could barely restrain himself from continuing his rush up the remaining stairs to Elizabeth's side to determine it for himself. A moment of dread washed over him when the serving girl hesitated. "What is it?" he demanded, fear lending a sharpness that he could not repress.

Panic-stricken, Ellen looked to the housekeeper. "Please, Mrs. Reynolds, that was all I was to say!"

"There, girl," the housekeeper stepped up. "Just tell the master what you know, that is all." She nodded calmly to Darcy. "It's likely they never let her in the room for long, sir, young as she is."

"Of course," Darcy stepped away, allowing the girl to recover herself.

"Now, Ellen. As far as you know, Mrs. Darcy is in no distress or danger? You saw or heard no sign of such a thing, did you?" Mrs. Reynolds prompted her gently.

"No, ma'am, no 'un said that the mistress was in a bad way." She paused and then added the only information to which she was privy. "T'were a lot of blood, though! I took the sheets to the laundry myself."

"Well, there always is, girl." The housekeeper signalled that she was to take her leave and turned to Darcy with calm assurance. "It's true, sir, there always is. To my mind, there is every indication that all is very well."

Reynolds, who had stayed back from the exchange, came forward and bowed. "Please accept the sincere congratulations of the staff, sir." A broad smile creased his old, loyal face. "A great day for Pemberley, indeed!"

"Indeed! Thank you, Reynolds," Darcy responded automatically, his emotions still shredded by his fear for Elizabeth and the image of the soiled sheets.

The sound of rattling dishes advancing up the stairs from the kitchen recalled them. "Ah, here is some tea while you wait, sir. Might you like it in the library?" Mr. Reynolds suggested.

The required half an hour rein upon Darcy's impatience to behold with his own eyes a future sown in love and hope was endured with only small assistance from the tea tray. In truth, he could not contain himself long enough to enjoy either tea or cake. "A son!" he exclaimed aloud to the empty room, an irrepressible smile spreading across his face.

Looking about him in exaltation, he became suddenly aware of the family history that surrounded him. His mind leapt to what must have taken place in this very room almost thirty years ago and the consummate joy that his own birth must have caused his own beloved father. Happiness was tempered momentarily with a pang of longing.

That Father and Mama could have shared this day! He could almost see them. Father would have seized him by the shoulders with a glad cry of "Well done, my boy!" and Mama would have held out her arms to him in joy.

"Yes, a son, Father!" With an involuntary laugh, his mood lightened as he imagined their shared delight in the advent of their first grandson and a new generation of Darcys of Pemberley. A son to inherit Pemberley, he thought. A son to guide into all that being a Darcy of Pemberley meant and grow worthy of its care.

The jumble of his emotions at these new impressions caused the cup and saucer to shake and be laid aside in favour of pacing the room, his anxious thoughts shifting to Elizabeth. Was all truly well? Had Mrs. Reynolds been unduly reassuring? She had not, after all, been present at the birth. With each round of the room, his attention was arrested by the hands on the Sevres clock, their interminably slow advance tightening his anxiety with each tick.

Finally, a knock on the library door sounded, and a smiling Reynolds entered the room. "The Mistress and the young master are ready to receive you, sir."

Blessed relief coursed through Darcy, and with a laugh, he strode quickly to his wife's bedside.

"Here, Ma'am." Annie Fletcher sat her down gently at the dressing table and reached for a towel. The warm sponge bath had been so welcome, easing the strains of labour with each stroke. Now, clothed in a fresh nightgown, Elizabeth felt revived until she looked into the mirror, her wet hair trailing about her face and shoulders like some rain- bedraggled child.

"Annie, I still look a fright!"

"Surely not, Ma'am," Annie replied calmly. "Just let me dry and braid your hair. I promise Mr. Darcy will not be allowed in until you are quite ready to receive him."

Elizabeth closed her eyes, surrendering to her maid's gentle ministrations, the quiet of the room, and the miraculous disappearance of the pains which had wracked her body for so many hours. The swish of the door opening behind her made her jump and try to turn.

"Just the maid coming to make up the bed." Annie turned her mistress back to the mirror and took up the comb to prepare to braid.

Elizabeth looked up at Annie's reflection, her face anxious. "Did you see the baby? Did everything seem right? He was whisked away before I truly—"

Her maid paused in the dressing and smiled back. "Only a glimpse, Ma'am. Nurse seems to be well satisfied and has him in hand, so you should not worry yourself. He's beautiful," she added and resumed her braiding. "There, done! Let's have you take a turn about the room. Mrs. Roseby left orders that you should walk as much as you can."

"Oh, did she?" Elizabeth groaned as Annie helped her rise. After a few breaths, she made her way to the windows, passing from one to another to look out upon the effects of the night's storm. Pemberley's lake, frozen solid, glowed in the dusk of early evening. She marvelled again at the efficiency of the estate's servants, for it had already been swept clear and ringed with mounds of the snow ... deep snow that continued past the meadow and bowed low the trees of the park. *No skating for you,* she grimaced, recalling the skating parties of her first winter at Pemberley. Her next thoughts were distressing ones: *There is so much! Will Jane be able to come?*

The chamber maid approached and curtsied. "The bed is ready, Ma'am."

"Thank you, Ellen. Please tell Nurse we are ready." Elizabeth nodded her dismissal and turned back to the bed. All trace of the last fourteen hours of travail were gone, replaced by fresh, inviting blankets and quilts. But it was the excitement of at last holding her infant son for a minute and conducting a loving examination of him that propelled her to the bed. Annie plumped the pillows and helped her ease down onto the warmed sheets. A knock sounded, followed by the entrance of Nurse with a smile and swaddled bundle. Gently she lay the heir of Pemberley into Elizabeth's outstretched arms.

Was he truly beautiful? Elizabeth's experience of new-born infants was such that the appellation of "beautiful" was, more often than not, a conclusion of the eyes of a fond beholder rather than a disinterested observer. Carefully, she pushed aside the swaddling and looked into the surprisingly alert eyes of her little son. Her heart melted and she leaned in to place a gentle kiss on his forehead. Absolutely beautiful!

"Shall I send down for the Master, Ma'am?" Annie asked, happy tears in her eyes. "My man Fletcher says he'll not wait much longer no matter what Mrs. Roseby says."

"Yes, oh yes!" Elizabeth exclaimed softly. "He must come at once."

In a very short while, loud, rapid footsteps were heard from the hall that could only belong to her husband. Oddly, they ceased at the door for several heartbeats. Silence. Elizabeth and Annie looked at each other, puzzled. Quietly, the handle turned and with uncharacteristic hesitancy, the master of Pemberley entered the one room of his estate which for too many hours had been barred to him.

Darcy knew he would never forget this, his first sight of Elizabeth and their son nestled in loving communion in the midst of their marriage bed. In truth, he could barely breathe and was only vaguely aware of Annie Fletcher's parting curtsey. Then, when she passed by him into the hall, the spell that had overpowered him faded and the draw to their side insistent.

"You are well, my love?" Darcy asked, rounding the bed and carefully sitting opposite her. He scanned her face for the truth, no matter what she might say.

"Yes, very well," she assured him. Seeing the rise of his brows at her quick answer, she laughed quietly. "Yes, I am, even considering what came before this little one's entrance into the world. It truly is forgotten!" She loosened her hold on the sweet bundle and, laying him on the blanket between them, began to unwrap the swaddling. "Come and see your son."

"Stay a moment." Darcy's hand cupped Elizabeth's face and lifting it, he tenderly kissed her forehead, the tip of her nose, and finally her lips where he rested for some moments in love, profound relief, and deep thanksgiving.

Chapter 2

Wednesday, December 15, 1813

Little Alexander George Fitzwilliam Darcy, the "Young Master," as he was quickly christened by the servants, made his presence immediately known in the halls of his ancestral estate. His influence upon everything and everyone who had to do with Pemberley, from his own nursery maid to the farthest tenant's hearth-side, was quite in reverse proportion to his diminutive size.

"To be sure," responded Mrs. Reynolds to her master's exasperation with his heir's effect upon the efficiency of his household, "it is only to be expected. There's been no babe at Pemberley since Miss Georgiana's birth eighteen year ago! We are, all of us, a-twitter, sir." She paused at his irritated sigh and glance at the cold tea and—*could that be burnt toast*? "But we shall come about." She dropped her curtsey. "And I'll have a fresh pot brought up...a *hot*, fresh pot, sir."

Noticing her use of naval cant and wishing to soften his display of bad humour, Darcy recalled her. "Mrs. Reynolds, your grandson is home from the sea, is he?"

"Yes, sir," she replied, turning back with a broad smile. "*The Harrier* arrived at Portsmouth three days ago, and we'll have him home for several weeks. Long enough for Christmas and New Year, sir." She curtsied again.

"Just so," he responded to her happy news and nodded his dismissal. But when the breakfast room door closed behind his housekeeper, he could not repress another sigh and a shake of his head. With the excitement of Alexander's birth three days ago coming hard upon Christmas season, his household was at such sixes and sevens that he was heartily glad of his decision that this year Pemberley would take a holiday, as it were, from being the county's focus in its celebration.

As much as last Christmas had been truly magical, with Elizabeth at his side for her first Pemberley Christmas, his Matlock relations gathered round along with his wife's Aunt and Uncle Gardner and other select friends, entertaining guests *and* the country-side on a Christmas scale this year was a great deal too much to ask of anyone. He knew he was tired – Elizabeth certainly was, as well as in need of quiet – and the rest of his people, it appeared, needed to get accustomed to the presence of a baby at Pemberley.

"A-twitter!" he snorted, shaking his head.

This year the guest list would be quite circumscribed and in this, the snow of the past week was in their favour. His cousin Richard, posted to northern Spain to serve under Lt. General Sir John Hope, was rather too engaged and would be sorely missed. Only the Bingleys, who had arrived the day after Alexander's birth, Lord and Lady Matlock, freshly returned just the day before from

London with Georgiana, would brave the weather and gather to celebrate the nativities of his little son and of Christ Our Lord.

His in-laws, Mr. and Mrs. Bennet, had sent their profound regrets that they and their daughters who yet remained at home would not be able to make the snowy journey despite Mrs. Bennet's anxiety to hold her first grandchild in her arms while gazing upon the grandeurs of Pemberley. In a welcome postscript, his father-in-law had peremptorily declined any assistance for a journey to Derbyshire, writing that the ecstasies of his wife could be postponed until Pemberley was in better frame to withstand them.

"*Yes*," thought Darcy with satisfaction as the fresh tea and toast made its appearance, "*I suppose that we shall 'come about.'*"

None of his family had yet joined him—it was a bit early for a winter's morn—but when he rose to refill his plate at the sideboard, he heard light steps approaching from the hall. The breakfast room door opened to reveal the welcome countenance of his sister. Stepping into the room, Georgiana met him with a smile and a kiss. "Good morning, Brother," she greeted him brightly.

"Georgiana," he returned, mirroring her smile. "Rather early for you after such a journey. But not unwelcome," he hastened to add. "I have missed your company at breakfast these past months…and such stylish company," he added with a nod to her morning gown of Dutch Blue superfine wool, the decorative silver lace framing her face in a most pleasing manner.

She laughed and sketched him a curtsey before turning to choose her repast. "Thank you, Fitzwilliam. One of the many things I have learnt in London: one must be 'up to the mark' at all times, if not exceeding it...even at breakfast. And who knows what the London servants might gossip abroad if the latest touchstone of fashion is not being meticulously observed?" She brought her plate to the table as Darcy poured her tea.

"Gossip?" He almost flinched at the word, the events at Ramsgate two years ago brought suddenly to mind. Steadying himself, he looked at her with guarded interest over his lifted cup.

"You were quite right in cautioning me, Fitzwilliam. Gossip and rumour are London's bread and butter! It is so very...irritating," she declared, "and silly! Even at concerts and lyceums, where one hoped for thoughtful conversation, it is all scandal and triviality."

Darcy released his held breath. "London has disappointed, then?"

Georgiana pursed her lips in consideration. "That is what Lord Brougham asked."

"Brougham! And how did you answer him?"

"That, as yet, I could not say. Certainly, there is some cause for discontent with the life in London I have experienced since my introduction at Court."

"All those boring balls—" Darcy teased. "I sympathize entirely."

"No, no, Brother!" Georgiana laughed, her countenance clearing momentarily. "The balls and new gowns in which to attend them are, I confess, quite exciting—most of the time. It is the, ah... *attention* I receive that is often difficult to deal with both in amount and degree. You remember how it was in April?"

Darcy nodded. Georgiana's introduction into Society had caused rather a large ripple in the Beau Monde, as he had known it would. His hands had been quite full with the immediate deluge of suitors— few of them worthy— and presenting himself to the mavens of the *ton* in order to secure the requisite invitations and tickets for the Season. It had been daunting and even alarming at times to a young woman of Georgiana's modest temperament and a gauntlet for his own equanimity.

He almost shuddered at the memory and thanked Heaven once more for his aunt. For last Christmas, Lady Matlock—bless her—had proposed to conduct Georgiana's entire coming out. A native in a world in which his own Elizabeth had little entrée or experience, his aunt proceeded to plan, then navigate the myriad social intricacies of a young lady's introduction into Society's ranks. When, mere weeks after his sister's court introduction, Elizabeth discovered that she was in an interesting condition, it had appeared especially providential. Illness peculiar to that condition recommended that Elizabeth return to Pemberley. He'd accompanied her home but returned to London for the remainder of the Season, forced to content himself with letters and short visits home.

"Did you say as much to Lord Brougham?" he asked.

"Yes, but he was often a witness to my discomfort, so he understood completely."

"Ah." Darcy waited for the rest. He *had* asked his friend Dyfed Brougham, Earl of Westmarch, to keep an eye upon her, or rather on the drones of Society which swarmed about her. In truth, Dy was likely more aware than himself concerning which aspirants to Georgiana's hand required polite but firm and immediate discouragement. Dy also possessed the means to discreetly inquire about any whose reputation or family history was unknown to him.

Means and motivation, he reminded himself. Dy had served him in this before, with skill and delicacy, during his visit two years ago to his Aunt Catherine in Kent. *Who better than his greatest friend and an agent of His Majesty to keep her safe? It was just that other madness...*

"'Understanding' is one of Lord Brougham's long suits," he ventured after several moments of silence. "He was of service to you often, then?"

"He is your very good friend." Georgiana's reply echoed his thoughts but its circumspection did not satisfy his curiosity. "And I am ever so grateful for his 'understanding' *and* advice." She patted her brother's hand and smiled sweetly. "Now, how are Elizabeth and little Alexander this morning?"

Before Darcy could pursue the matter, the door was opened to admit another to breakfast. "Good morning, Charles. You slept well; I trust?"

"As may be," his friend Bingley responded with a yawn. "Likely not much better than you." He took up a plate and advanced upon the sideboard. "Jane attends your wife in her dressing room whenever your son decides he is hungry—which is always." Darcy saluted him with his fork in agreement and emitted a rueful laugh.

"Good practice and fair warning, I suppose. In two months, it shall be our turn." He set his plate down, sat, and reached for the teapot. "Good morning to you also, Georgiana." He took a gulp of the tea and continued, "You are up early for having just arrived from London yesterday. Not how my sisters respond to traveling, to be sure!"

"Good morning to you! I am sorry you had a fitful night."

"Well, babies are like that at the beginning, so I am told. I *was* starting to wonder the third time," Bingley replied. "He is a Darcy, you know!"

"Oh, surely—"Georgiana protested, then broke into a laugh when she spied Bingley's broad wink.

Darcy ignored his friend's jibe. "Mrs. Reynolds has informed me that Pemberley is 'all a-twitter' with the boy. So, it may be cold tea and burnt toast as well as fitful nights until we all become accustomed to him."

Bingley lifted his tea cup, a question upon his face.

"Second pot," Darcy explained and turned to his sister. "What shall you do today?"

Chapter 3

Late that afternoon, another storm howled through Derbyshire, setting the old men to muttering ominously into their cups at The Green Man. Unlike the Black Mare's Head across Lambton's main thoroughfare, The Green Man braved the storm and remained open into the evening. The inn's lanterns spoke of welcome through the swirls of snow but its hospitality consisted this night in only a thin stew that bubbled with half a heart to the side of a fire needed to warm the taproom as well. Wood for any purpose was precious this season. Winters of the past decade had been cold, of course, but not burdened with such an excess of snow. Local woodcutters were hard pressed to replace what was fast burning up in weather that made their paths into the forest passible one day and impossible the next.

But the Green Man still had a good supply of ale. The landlord's mother-in-law, plagued by troubling dreams that summer, would not be quieted until she prevailed over his growls that the cost of enlarging his brewery would be ruinous. Her nightmare fears had served them well. They were still open, coins clinked on the bar, and custom from the less fortunate Black Mare's Head were, for the time being, his.

Then, against all expectation, the sounds of an approaching team of horses penetrated the taproom. Curiosity high, several men rushed to the windows and then exclaimed to the host that a coach had pulled up at the very door.

"What daft—?" the landlord frowned, but quickly replaced it with a smile as the door swung open. A man, likely the driver, stepped inside. His hand still on the knob and snow falling from his capes and hat, he quickly surveyed the astonished room, noted the fire, nodded to the landlord approaching him and left. The room exploded with questions and exclamations, but those at the window called out, "He's openin' the coach door!"

"Aye, looks like a gent'man. Two gen...no, t'other's his man, most like."

"Who'd be out in this weather? He must come ten mile!"

"Making his driver and them horses..."

The door opened again, admitting the "gentleman," his companion, and the driver, who forcefully advanced upon the landlord before he'd even a hope of bowing his welcome. "A table near the fire for my lord," he barked, "such as it is, and be quick about it. And a brick for the coach, nay—two, we leave momentarily," he added.

The room was astonished. They were going back out...in *this* weather?

"Yes, yes of course," the host finished his bow and signalled those at the afore mentioned table to clear away in favour of the new arrival. "But surely you will stay!" The driver's curled lip and disdainful look about him disabused his host of that possibility. "At least rest...warm yourselves and let us see to your cattle!" He looked beyond the driver to the nobleman. "My Lord?"

"Grayson," his lordship stepped past his driver as he shrugged off his greatcoat into the arms of his valet. "We can afford a few minutes and more—some civility to our host." The young lord smiled apologetically and addressed the landlord. "Might there be someone who would water the horses, and a little feed, perhaps? Just a little, and then keep them moving? We really cannot stay long."

"Immediately, my lord." Another signal and the two ostlers bolted for the door, eager to uphold the honour of the Green Man if not to brave the cold. "Please, come to the fire," Garston bowed again, "and have something warm to drink."

"Thank you, my good man," his lordship replied and followed him to the hearth where he stood before the humble fire without ceremony.

While the host warmed servings of his best libation at the same hearth, he took the measure of the young man standing nearby. *Young! Yes, likely mid-twenties, handsome countenance, strong bearing...and not high in the instep! At least, not at the moment. But the driver! Hmm...* He looked over at the valet who had said nothing and now was arranging his master's greatcoat on a chair and easing it to the hearth. *Too busy to tell naught 'bout him except he knows his business.* He brought the mugs up to the table, checking for crumbs and wet spots. Pulling out his towel from his waist, he gave the table a final polish and waited beside it for his lordship. *Who is he and where's a stranger goin' on such a night in such a hurry?*

"My lord," he pulled out the chair.

His lordship looked up from an intense scrutiny of the fire. "Ah, no." He stepped over and chose a mug of steaming drink, saluting his host before taking a draught. "Ahh." He swallowed and closed his eyes. "No offense to your hospitality, landlord," he apologized again, "but it has been a long journey." His voice was pleasant—deep, but not overly so. Most of all, the landlord noticed the tiredness in his shadowed blue eyes and the smile that again flashed but now quickly faded.

His driver came to the table. "My lord, the horses?"

"Excuse me, my lord," the landlord hastened to bow himself into the conversation. "We have fine cattle with which to relieve yours. You will not be put to the blush at your destination, I assure you. Your horses will be very well cared for and delivered to you in a few days if, as you say, you will not be far from Lambton."

"My lord?" his driver asked again, his face carefully blank. The landlord, though, thought he detected something, but he could not name it.

The question animated the valet as well. He straightened from his stance at the hearth. "My lord, your fa—

"Yes," his lordship forestalled him with flashing eyes. "I am *well* aware."

"Grayson," his lordship turned then to his driver, "have yourself a mug and then go see how they fare. I think one has picked up a stone." With a nod, the driver obeyed and took up a mug, but headed with it for the door instead. Then he regarded his valet, who, like the driver, the host guessed, had some twenty years on their master. His lordship addressed him in wearied tone. "You also, Magus, drink up, then bespeak the bricks. We cannot be too far, but I will not have you or Grayson freeze."

"Yes, my lord." The valet bowed, took up the last mug, and retreated to the kitchen in evident relief.

His people set about their duties; the young man turned to his host. "I am in no doubt that your stock is exceptional," he prefaced his tight response, "but with regret, I must decline." With this, he sat down heavily and turned his face again to the fire.

Not too far?' Beside himself with curiosity at every aspect of this night's arrival, the landlord struggled not to ask what the whole room thirsted to know. *Where were they going? What would this young lord, or his more experienced driver, call 'Not too far*?' Garston mentally rifled through the catalogue of villages and their estates which were within reasonable distance but could only shrug his shoulders at his customers.

With the nobleman's silence and their host's confoundment, there was no more to amaze the regulars of The Green Man. They went back to their ale. Some spoke of heading for home, but most of them were reluctant to leave the curious scene until all was played and the strangers were on their mad way into the snowy night.

A quarter of an hour passed without movement from the hearthside table, although some said they heard occasional sighs. Then, some stamping of boots at the door heralded the return of the driver, causing everyone to look to it for the next part in the evening's drama. A gust of wind blew him in; everyone looked carefully away even as all ears were pitched.

"Ready, my lord," he bellowed. With a quick bow in his direction, he went to the kitchen in search of the valet and, it was supposed, to secure the heated bricks.

His lordship rose from his chair. "You have been most attentive, landlord, but we can enjoy your hospitality no longer. We must be off." The last was said with determination, as if a task had been handed him that only now was fully embraced.

Or, perhaps, thought Garston, *it is only the snow and the night.*

His lordship's valet hurried to him. Lifting his greatcoat from the chair, he shook it out and held it ready, "My lord." He slipped it onto his lord's waiting frame and made to work the buttons but was waived away. "Your hat, my lord."

"Thank you, Magus." He then looked significantly at his valet, then the landlord, and then walked out the door.

The valet quickly pulled on his own coat and a shawl and hat, also left by the fire.

Reaching into a pocket, he pulled out a purse. He peered inside it and shook out some coins into his hand. Biting his lip, he considered them for a moment with lowered eyes. He chose but one, laid it quickly on the table and followed his master into the night. In moments, the sound of the harness and creak of the coach announced that the strangers were departing the inn yard for the road.

With that, the native curb of the Green Man's customers in the company of gentry or lord evaporated as a drop of water on a skillet.

"What was that? One coin only?" a customer exclaimed.

"I should hope it's a crown," another put in.

Garston quickly palmed the coin and shoved it into his pocket. "Never you mind." Regardless of his tone, the crowd could see that he strove to control disappointment. The landlord's good wife appeared at the kitchen door with a tray full of clean glasses and mugs and her mind full of questions.

"Who *was* that, husband?" she asked, setting down the tray on the bar.

"His man only left a half-crown," a neighbour informed her before her husband could say a word.

"In truth?" she cast him a look of disbelief.

"It was his man what paid," he replied, after giving his neighbour a warning glare. "Could be his lordship meant more, but the valet held back. That *all* could see!" His tone of voice dared anyone to disagree. *One never knew,* he reasoned, *but the mysterious lord might come through again and in a better frame.* "The Green Man has a good reputation and defames no guest," he loudly reminded his customers. *And no use killing a goose that might lay an egg my way in the future.*

The glasses and mugs were almost all shelved when the ostlers banged through the door, shivering so much their teeth chattered, and made for the hearth. The crowd made way for them, the landlord hard on their heels. Clapping them on their backs he leaned into them, drawing them close. Every ear strained to hear what they answered to his whispered inquiry, but it wasn't long before the whole room knew.

"Pemberley!" the landlord exclaimed. "Why did they even stop!"

"Didn't know the way, sir," they answered. "Knew Lambton, but not where Pemberley lay." Neighbour looked at neighbour in disbelief. Pemberley was less than five miles away!

The younger ostler pulled at the landlord's sleeve and motioned him back into close communication. "That driver, sir, he's a deep 'un!"

"What do you mean?"

"He asked for our heaviest hammer. Said sumptin 'ad shaken loose an' he needed to fix it. Well, sir, he never did return that hammer. It's clean gone. Jus' wanted you to know, sir."

"If they didn't know the way!" Garston's wife reasoned loudly, "and Pemberley didn't send to warn that anyone was coming who *didn't* know the way...they can't be expected!" She continued in a lower voice, "We know for certain sure that *strangers* ain't expected because of the Young Master. Most all Christmas not happenin' this year up Pemberley. Keep it quiet for the Mistress and babe." Her husband nodded and then shooed her back to the shelves. Some quiet of his own was needed to mull over this strange night.

Not expected! The Green Man fair rumbled with the words...words that could not but invite a storm of speculation.

Chapter 4

"Surely, he cannot continue on to York in this dreadful weather, Fitwilliam!" Elizabeth put a coaxing hand on her husband's arm. They were all gathered in the Blue Salon, having just sat before the fire to partake of Cook's celebrated iced fruitcake marking Elizabeth's release from childbed, when Reynolds came with the startling news.

Darcy looked up at her from his perusal of the letter of introduction in his hand. Her lovely smile threatened to melt his natural guard against such surprises as this evening's arrival at his front door of a young French nobleman quite unknown to him. "No, no of course not," his smile down at her was cautious. He looked over to his brother-in-law. "Charles, have you ever heard of the Comte du Pont-Courlay or his father, the Duc de Fronsac?"

"No," Bingley shrugged, shaking his head with a laugh. "My acquaintance does not usually extend to French nobility. But the letter; who is it from?"

"A fellow member of my club, Lord Deaveraux. He recommends him to my acquaintance in *unexceptional* terms."

"Deaveraux? Is he reliable?" Bingley left his wife's side and peered over Darcy's shoulder at the letter. "I do not know him well."

"He can be relied upon not to cheat at cards!" Darcy replied.

Bingley rolled his eyes and, after stifling a laugh, Elizabeth regarded her spouse primly. Darcy abandoned his sarcasm and returned to serious reflection. "Before Boodle's I knew him at university, although I was not in his set and he was three years before me. His family is old and well respected."

"Then a night's shelter cannot hurt." Elizabeth prompted.

"Hmm," Darcy murmured, looking over the formal document again. "It will be more than a night, my dear. The snow is quite deep and the damage that the Comte's coach has suffered will not easily be mended."

Georgiana rose and joined her brother. "The snow! It is miraculous that they got as far as they did! I doubt that even my aunt and uncle will arrive at Pemberley when they had planned, and they come only from Matlock."

"Miraculous...yes," Darcy repeated, regarding his sister. "*You* do not recall meeting the Comte? Danced with him in London or a house party, perhaps?"

"No, Brother, I recall being introduced to no such person. The few *émigrés* I encountered were older gentlemen and they did not dance nor seek introduction to young ladies." She turned to Elizabeth. "They were more interested in political introductions." Her young face grew pensive. "Shadows flitting along ballroom walls. Sad, really."

"Eh-hem," Reynolds ventured with delicacy to interrupt the discussion, "Our guest has sent that he is ready to join you, sir."

"Fitzwilliam, we cannot think of sending the Comte away until *everything* has been repaired and the weather improves. After all, it is Christmas!" Georgiana pled.

"I was not about to order the servants drive him from our door," he teased her and kissed her forehead, "but only because it *is* Christmas." She shook her head at him in a mock disapproval that ended in the amusement Darcy had intended. "As for the rest, we shall see. Reynolds," he directed the butler, "you may conduct the Comte here to us."

Darcy turned and taking his wife by the hand, conducted her back to the settee. "I cannot like this," he murmured to her as, with a sigh, she settled into it.

"Are you well?" Her sigh alarmed him. "Is this too much?"

"No, no. I am just a little tired from standing and need only to sit down." Elizabeth assured him. "Besides, I would not miss all this excitement for the world! Who would have thought: a stranger—a Comte, no less—arrives in distress on the eve of a snowy night at Christmastide?"

"Yes, who would have thought?" Darcy straightened with a frown and pulled at his waistcoat. "I would have preferred to meet him alone first, not in the midst of family and only on Deaveraux's introduction.

"He'll be charming," Elizabeth predicted, "but I can see in what direction your concern truly lies." She nodded past him to Georgiana. "She will—

The salon door opened. "The Comte du Pont-Courlay," Reynolds solemnly announced to the room. They all rose as Darcy strode forward to receive this unexpected guest.

"Comte," he bowed. "Welcome to Pemberley."

Standing behind her brother and sister-in-law, Georgiana had little opportunity to observe their guest before dropping her eyes and performing the deep curtsey his rank required. When she arose, it was only to have her equanimity shaken to its core. Her eyes widened and she involuntarily stepped back. He looked...*he looked an angel!*

Quickly, she averted her gaze and pinched her wrist. *How utterly ridiculous!*

What are you thinking! But of their own accord, her eyes flew back to him as her brother began the introductions.

Crowned by golden brown curls that fell over a high brow, the Comte's upright, well-formed person bespoke his noble breeding. His lively blue eyes and delicately arched brows beamed with honest pleasure at his host and all them around him. A straight nose and mobile lips that easily curved in good humour in a pale but healthy countenance completed a picture that, indeed, echoed the angelic that Georgiana had seen in countless galleries.

She could feel her cheeks warm with confusion at her untoward reaction. She dropped her eyes. How she should ever speak to him...look at him?

"My wife, Mrs. Darcy." Elizabeth stepped forward and prepared to curtsey again, but the Comte forestalled her.

"*Non, non, Madame!* Do not trouble yourself. It is too much," he took her hand and bowed over it. "It is I who have imposed upon your so lovely family. *Infâme! Pardon,* s'il vous plaît."

Almost against her will, Georgiana acknowledged that his voice was melodious and... kind. His dress also recommended him to her. He did not follow the height of fashion: his collar was not in the extreme of London beaux nor was the fall of ruffles from his cravat excessive. The dark green velvet of his coat, worn over a simple but elegantly embroidered silver waistcoat, was certainly rich; but he wore them with a nonchalance that absolved him of any subtle play of rank.

"My sister, Miss Georgiana Darcy." Her brother quickly took possession of her hand, tucking it against his side. *Was it relief that he had done so, or was it annoyance that was warming her cheeks once more?* Her disconcertion. She could not look at him.

"*Enchanté, Mademoiselle.*" He paused for her response, some polite welcoming phrase.

Surely, you can manage simple words of greeting! All the conversation of her London season disserted her.

"The room, it is quite warm; is it not?" the Comte supplied quietly, without a hint of condescension.

Kind. Again, the impression offered itself and it gave her the presence of mind to look up at him. The smile she found there called forth her own.

"Yes, my lord," she managed to respond, "but it must be quite welcome after being stranded in such a storm."

"*Certainement!*" His encouraging smile transformed into one of pleasure. He looked to the entire salon. "*Mais s'il vous plaît,* you have rescued me and cannot be forever 'my lord this' and 'my lord that' during this, our time together. *Permettez-moi.*" He bowed before them. "You have the letter, no? But more, I introduce myself: André Eugène Reynard St.-Sébastien. Since I am named after my beloved Grandpère, I am called from childhood, Bastien."

"Charles Bingley," Bingley stepped forward, hand extended. "If we may introduce ourselves, that is. And this is my wife Jane, Mrs. Darcy's sister."

"Madame Bingley, *enchanté.*"

"Shall you like some refreshment, my lo—pardon me, Bastien?" Elizabeth motioned to the table laden with fruitcake, coffee, and other enticements. "Georgiana, would you—?"

"Or a drink first, perhaps," Darcy interjected, releasing Georgiana's hand. "Charles?"

She watched as her brother shepherded the two gentlemen to another table across the room.

Bastien, she mused, trying out the name in her mind as she followed their progress and then engage in the rituals of gentleman and drink. Lifting his glass, her brother's gaze suddenly met hers and brought her back to herself with a start.

Oh! He must not see me staring! She turned quickly to the refreshments and chose a piece of fruitcake, bringing an errant dab of frosting to her lips before turning to Elizabeth and Jane. She joined them, sitting beside Elizabeth, whose warm presence would surely ground her...keep her thoughts from straying.

Bastien... André Eugène Reynard St.-Sébastien. Hmm, she pondered. *What was it about him that turned her speechless, graceless, and into the veriest ninny? The kind of simpering Miss she could not bear?*

"Georgiana?" Elizabeth whispered close by her ear, "Is something amiss, dear?"

"I...no, no," she stuttered, dismayed that the emotions she struggled to understand were so easily displayed. She cast Elizabeth a faint smile and motioned to her plate. "Is not this cake delicious? What are the spices, do you think?"

Elizabeth's brow rose. "Cinnamon...and ginger, surely," she replied slowly, studying her face. "Perhaps, a little nut—"

"Nutmeg! Yes, it must be the nutmeg." Georgiana's voice rose, then quickly trailed off into silence. Finishing her cake, she picked up her embroidery from the basket set nearby and bent to her work even while her attention lay across the room. She could hear the men talking but, frustratingly, could only wonder what was being said.

The embroidery pattern was all French knots at this juncture, and she should have known not to attempt them in her distracted state. At the third tangled stitch, she let the hoop drift onto her lap. *Embroidery! No fit distraction for a distracted mind*! she quipped to herself. Elizabeth had turned to her sister and the two were preoccupied, laughing quietly over something that one of them had said.

Georgiana's gaze strayed back to the men. Something had come to an end, for glasses were being laid aside and slow steps made toward the ladies.

"Bastien, Charles," Darcy indicated chairs as they approached the women before the fire.

"*Merci*," the Comte sighed as he sank into a chair near Georgiana. "It has been a very long day."

"You must tell us the rest of your story!" Bingley pulled his chair up closer. "Ladies, you must hear this! It is quite shocking!"

"Only if you wish to tell it." Elizabeth turned a curious eye upon the Comte. "We would not wish to cause you pain."

"Ah, *Madame*, it is not so uncommon a tale in these days if you are acquainted with *la Révolution. Mais si vous le souhaitez*, if you wish, I will begin again and then, as Charles has kindly requested, I will finish."

Chapter 5

My father is Armand Henri Emmanuel de St. Sébastien, le Duc de Fronsac. Our primary estate— our château— is in the *Bordeaux*. You know *Bordeaux*, yes?" He looked to them all for affirmation, but his eyes paused until Georgiana nodded.
"I should think!" Bingley responded. "Wine country!"
"*Oui*, the wine country. Our *Bouchet* grapes have been grown there since the days of the Romans. *Alors*, I was born at the château and not yet three years old when *le Duc*, my father, was called to *Paris* for *le Estates General*. He brought us all, *ma mère* and my older sister also, for he feared the countryside even then and did not want to be parted from us. You know what occurred," he shrugged his shoulders and shook his head, his brow furrowed. "The unrest, the *Bastille*... We could not return home or even leave our house in the city."
"How awful for you," cried Jane.
"I cannot remember, *Madame* Bingley. I was too young," he replied solemnly. "But the stories of those times have been told again and again in my family." His voice caught. He rose and stood at the fire for a few moments to compose himself. "It became too dangerous in *Paris*. Laws were broken by the mob with impunity." He turned back to them. "The homes of my father's

friends were attacked, some burned. He decided then, like so many others, that it was time to flee. We became *émigrés* in Austria for several years."

"When was that?" Darcy asked.

"From 1789 until 1792, when the *Assembly* threatened Austria with war if they did not give us up."

"What did you do?" Georgiana blurted out, transfixed by the Comte's narrative.

His expressive countenance fell, "Ah, *Mademoiselle* Darcy, we fled again. To Switzerland, Prussia, Denmark, anywhere my father had relatives or friends..." He paused, surveying his audience, "...but more often, to other *émigrés* with plans *impossible* to overthrow *la République*. It was during those years that *ma mère* and *ma sœur* became ill and passed into a better world." He quickly crossed himself and kissed his fingers to Heaven.

Resuming his seat, he gripped the chair's arms so tightly that Georgiana, even with tear dimmed eyes, could see the cords standing out in his hands. Carefully, she raised her gaze to his face. His attention was focused on the fire, his bearing the very embodiment of nobility and loss. Something stirred within her and in that moment, Georgiana could no more halt the wave of compassion that flooded over her than stop the sea. In a rush, her heart went out to him.

Eager for the rest, Bingley broke the silence. "—And then came Napoleon!"

"*Oui*, then came Napoleon," the Comte sighed. He collected himself and cast upon them all a sad smile. "And all the years of *émigré* plotting came to nothing.

Not at first, of course, but as his power grew and he became *l'idole des rues*..." His hand became a fist. "*Mon père* has resigned himself—'We must rely on the great powers such as England to regain our country, our place in the world again,' he now says." He fell silent once more.

"So, now you are in England," Darcy prompted. "Traveling into York?"

An underlying tone in her brother's question arrested Georgiana's attention. She examined the dispassionate lines of his face and glanced quickly to the others. It had not been noticed! They all continued to look in sympathy upon their guest. *Could she be mistaken?* She looked back to her brother, and saw now a glint of wariness in his eyes. *Not mistaken! Why?* She looked down at the embroidery which still lay in her lap, her emotions in a like tangle of disorder, and listened for the Comte's reply.

"To an estate in the vicinity that has welcomed my father's interest." His countenance lightened a little. "I answer his summons to determine, is it suitable? The time to come to terms is short. Others are interested. This accident! *Malheureux*...most unfortunate. I cannot thank you enough, *Monsieur*..."

Rapt again in his narrative, Georgiana almost jumped when Elizabeth laid a hand upon her arm. "I think it is time to check on little Alexander. Would you be so kind as to lend me your arm and your company? I find myself more tired than I thought, and Fitzwilliam is occupied with our guest." She rose unsteadily. "I must take my leave first and I will include yours. Wait for me at the door, Georgie. I shall be there directly. Jane?"

"Take my arm, Lizzy," Jane commanded, rising with no more grace than her sister. "We'll waddle over together." She patted her blooming middle. "Two tired, fat old hens!" She laughed and winked at Georgiana. "You can take my place when we part in the hall."

"Yes, ma'am," she replied and curtsied before starting toward the salon door. *Dismissed!* But then she reconsidered. *Or shielded? And are you relieved or annoyed?* She sighed. *Or both?*

~~&~~

The bitter winds of the storm battering her windows had worn themselves to whispers while Georgiana's maid braided her hair for bed in the soft candle light of her dressing table.

"Will that be all, miss?"

"Yes, Barrow, thank you."

Her maid gathered up the London gown and petticoats she had worn that evening and closed her chamber door. Georgiana considered the dress. It had been perfect for a small family gathering, but it was not a one for making impressions.

If that was what one desired. She shook herself, trying to dismiss such thoughts, and drifted to a window overlooking the east meadow and the park beyond. The storm had whipped away the clouds and a waning crescent moon shone bravely in a wispy sky, lending a sparkling glaze to the snow-drifted scene below.

Angels we have heard on high,
Sweetly singing o'er the plain...

Georgiana sang softly, laying a hand on the upper sash, her forehead against the pane. Christmastide and snow under the moon never failed to bring this carol to mind. As she sang, she heard it in her mother's voice. Fitzwilliam had been dubious that it could be a true memory. She had been so young when their mother passed away! But, despite his scepticism, she had held to her conviction and cherished the soothing memory from long ago.

Gloria in excelsis Deo! She thought on that wish and then upon the young Comte come so curiously into her life.

Bastien, she named him in a whispered prayer to Heaven. *Into Your hands...*

~~&~~

"You are not coming to bed?" Elizabeth asked in surprise when her husband entered their bedchamber still dressed.

Darcy sat down wearily upon their bed and leaned over to kiss her. "No, I cannot sleep just yet," he sighed.

"*Le Comte?*" she guessed after returning his warm salute.

"*Certainement!*" he quipped with a haughty air, eliciting laughter from his beloved. "I *wish* that I could laugh!"

"And you cannot," she stated rather than asked. In their fourteen months as man and wife, she had come to know him well enough to gauge most of his moods.

"It is all too convenient!" he responded vehemently and rose from the bed. Going to the window, he peered out into the night. "At least the storm has subsided. The moon is out," he noted, then turned back to her. "What do you think?"

Elizabeth tried to stifle a yawn. "About the Comte or—

"Everything! Yes!"

"I was going to say 'about Georgiana.'"

Darcy stared at her and slowly let out the breath he was holding. "She is attracted to him..."

"And it alarms you." Elizabeth finished for him.

"It *all* alarms me," he confessed. "A man I do not know nor of whom I have heard suffers an accident at my gate during the snow storm of the decade—"

"You cannot fault him for the snow!" she interrupted.

"And the accident?" He paused, calming himself, then asked, "What of the Comte? I concede that his address is impeccable, his manner open."

"And he is beautiful!"

Darcy's lips twisted in a wry response. "He dresses well."

Elizabeth laughed again. "Yes, he dresses well," she mimicked him. "Fashionable... rich, but understated. His French accent does not hurt, either." Her husband's answering snort dissuaded her from pursuing that line. "But what most concerns you is not the Comte nor his coach, but Georgiana's response to him." Elizabeth hesitated, then continued delicately, "She is much moved by him."

"It is not like her!" he protested.

"No," she agreed, "but it may be...now."

~~&~~

Darcy took up the quill, then paused in the weak circle of light illuminating his desk. *More light.* He drew the candle closer, wishing he had another near at hand, but it was now very late and he desired this letter be on its difficult way at first light.

December 15
Pemberley House

Dy—
Something has arisen...

Chapter 6

Thursday, December 16, 1813

As soon as there was sufficient light, Darcy surprised his stablemaster with a summons to meet him at the carriage house. When the man arrived a quarter hour later with more than one question writ in his heavy-eyed face, Darcy handed him a lantern.

"Mr. Darcy?"

"Taylor." Darcy raised his own and motioned to him to follow as he spoke. "I want your help in examining our guest's entire coach from shaft to boot as well as all the harnessing."

"Sir, Harry and I were going to—"

"Good, do that. I want Harry's eyes and opinions as well, but he is away on an errand for me and will not return for some time. Ah, there it is." He turned down an aisle raising his lantern as they approached for a better view of the vehicle. When they were upon it, both men stopped and surveyed it in silence.

Taylor cast a questioning frown at his master. "It's severely damaged, for certain, sir, as we sent to you last night. Is it a list of repairs and parts you want? Harry'd be your man for that, sir."

"That will be later. Right now, I want your help in looking at the damage itself and bring to my attention anything that looks...hmm," he searched for a neutral term that would not excite suspicion, "unusual."

"Unusual, sir?"

"Not what you would expect...out of place. Start at the front; I'll come from the rear."

An hour later, the two men met in the middle of the coach. "Anything?" Darcy asked as he wiped his hands of dirt.

"Well, the first thing, sir, is the amount of damage. It is looking more far-reaching than I'd thought last night. Of course, that might not be 'unusual' as it was late, dark, and frankly, sir, cold as a—"

"Noted," Darcy nodded. "What next?"

"The locations and direction of the cracks and breaks, they don't entirely make sense to me, sir. But," he tracked backward hurriedly, "I'm not a carpenter nor a carriage maker." He lay a hand on the coach body. "I *can* say that this was a fine coach in its day."

"In its day?"

Taylor patted it, then withdrew his hand. "About thirty years old or more. French made, most likely. Made a'fore springs. Harry could tell you more."

"Hmm," Darcy responded and lapsed into silence, his eyes travelling the length of the vehicle and back. A shaft of morning light flashed through a window, causing the perpetual dust of a carriage house to dance before his eyes. He must get back to the house before his absence was noted.

"Thank you, Taylor." He handed him his lantern. "As soon as Harry returns, go over it with him again. You both should examine the horses as well and report to me when you are finished." He looked back at the coach. "And do not speak of this with anyone but Harry, before or after you come to me."

"Yes, sir," Taylor replied, pulling at his cap and taking the lantern.

As they were leaving, Darcy paused. "And Taylor, I would be very interested in anything the Comte's driver might say about the accident. No questions! Whatever he volunteers in passing and of his own accord." The stablemaster nodded his understanding and strode off to the stables.

Darcy turned back to Pemberley House and, for a few moments, watched the strengthening dawn tint its walls and windows with light. Looking then to the park, and the snow-choked drive that disappeared into the darkness of the wood, he strained to see what could not yet be there. A sharp breeze whistled through the stable yard and found him standing there. With a shiver, he hurried to the sun-gilded house. If he were quick, he could hope to share a few moments before breakfast with Elizabeth and his son.

Not wishing to encounter any of his guests, Darcy took a servant's entrance into the House. Clambering up the empty back stairs to the bedchamber floor, he entered his dressing room through the servant's door, pulling it softly behind him.

"Mr. Darcy, sir?"

Darcy whirled from the door to behold his valet where before there had been only empty air. "Fletcher! You startled me! Where the deuce—"

"In the coat closet, sir, determining where you might be from what is missing. I see I am correct, and you must have been about the stables."

"Close...the carriage house." He turned away from the curiosity in his valet's face and presented him his back.

"Of course, sir," Fletcher replied quietly and began removing the layers of worn clothing usually reserved for inspection tours with the steward. "Examining the Comte's coach, I imagine?"

Darcy peered over his shoulder. "You have met the Comte's valet?"

"Briefly, sir," he affirmed, tossing the coat over a chair. "Magus is the man's name, I believe, but that is the sum of my acquaintance at this point. Should you like me to discover in what corner the wind sits?"

"'Truth will out,'" Darcy shot back as the jacket and heavy scarf were whisked off to join the coat. "But as you do, remember the 'better part of valour.'"

"Discretion. As always, sir."

~~&~~

Georgiana's maid slipped her morning dress over her shoulders and arranged the fastenings with practiced hands. Her mistress shook out the folds and smoothed the bodice as she looked into her mirror. *Yes...modest and perhaps a little plain,* she thought, evaluating the effect which was then completely overset by the paisley

Norwich shawl her maid draped over her arms. *Well, the shawl will not be noticed at table.* She pushed an errant curl back into place and sat to choose earrings from a selection her maid set out. *Too much...just...there!* She found a simply wrought pair and handed them over.

"These, Barrow." *Perfect*, she thought, looking at the overall effect. *Nothing that would suggests a special interest. Merely, Miss Darcy, come to breakfast like any other morning.* Even as she assured herself that this was so, her heart began to beat rapidly when the clock struck, calling her down to breakfast.

Should she try to be before him—*would that betray eagerness?*

Or wait to arrive after—*and perhaps indicate you wished to make an entrance?* Or...

*Georgiana Darcy! S*he rose and swept through her chamber door, refusing to think on it any further.

~~&~~

The murmur of men's voices reached Georgiana even before the footman opened the breakfast room door. Any idea of arriving before the Comte was quite dashed. Taking a deep breath to calm the frisson of trepidation shivering her body, she reminded herself to smile and entered.

The gentlemen all rose, but it was only the Comte who bowed and remained standing until she took her seat. The responding curtsey such a gesture required helped her to keep her gaze averted but that he had bowed was enough to unbalance her. Rising, she quickly moved around the table, continuing to avoid looking at him, and sat at her brother's left.

"*Bonjour, Mademoiselle,*" he offered from across the table while a serving man poured her tea. "It is a fine morning, is it not? Much improved over last night."

His voice! Had she forgotten? Her hand shook ever so slightly as she lifted her tea cup.

Say something, silly girl!

Before she could answer him or even raise her eyes, Bingley seconded the Comte's pronouncement. "Very much improved, indeed! Last night was wicked, sir, wicked!"

"Bastien, *s'il vous plaît*...please!" the Comte reminded him gently.

"Of course." Bingley smiled with pleasure at the assurance that he was included in last night's invitation to familiarity. "You were about to tell us what happened."

"*Bien sûr*, although I cannot tell you much. We departed Lambton, the Green Man—you know it, yes?—after my driver looked for the problem with a horse. A stone, perhaps, in the hoof? I did not inquire what he found."

"You were not tempted to put up at the Green Man? It is a comfortable little inn," Darcy put in. "They would have accommodated you well. I fear that the loss of your custom did not make you friends in Lambton."

Her brother's close presence and wry tone emboldened her to raise her eyes from the study of her plate to Fitzwilliam's face. A quirk of his lips visible to her alone made her smile.

"*Je n'ai aucun doute,*" Bastien responded. "I have no doubt, but my driver believed it necessary we should continue."

Curiosity at this statement conveyed Georgiana's glance to the Comte's face before she could catch herself. He seemed to have been waiting for her to abandon her pose of inattention, for the gentle smile that greeted her, the bright invitation in his eyes, and the expressive curve of his brows, undid her.

All the self-possession she had acquired fled. Her heart again took up that strange rush and thud in her ears. His lips moved, but she could neither hear him nor read his well-formed lips.

What is he saying?

A sense of panic, which she had not felt in more than a year, began to rise. She fought to pull her gaze from him. *Concentrate,* she commanded herself, and to her heart, *Have done with this!*

Finally, she could drop her eyes and look instead to her surroundings. The normalities of the breakfast room steadied her and the table conversation once more became intelligible. *Had anyone noticed? Had he noticed?* She devoutly hoped not but refused to allow herself to dwell on it. Of far more concern was her loss of self-command.

A footman from the hall entered discreetly and after bowing, presented Darcy with a note. Her brother read it swiftly in silence. "He has only just returned?" The servant answered affirmatively. "Send him to the kitchen and then to my book room in half an hour."

"Yes, sir."

"News?" queried Bingley.

"The 'news' is that there is none," Darcy sighed. "My people have made little progress in clearing Pemberley's drive. I doubt they will get more than a lane to the gate until tomorrow!"

"Unless there is more snow," Bingley put in.

"Yes," Darcy repeated grimly, "unless there is more snow." He continued, "The word from Lambton is that no conveyance of any kind has passed through the village since the Comte's. The few men who have struggled in from outlying farms this morning have done so only from cruel necessity. They report seeing evidence for no one beyond their own tenancies."

"*Mon Dieu*, this is very bad." The Comte shook his head.

"You will not get to your appointment, I fear, even if another coach could be found." Darcy rose from the table. "A messenger might be sent, but even that will take more time than the terms you described. I am truly sorry, Bastien. You are quite stranded here."

"To be stranded at your Pemberley and in such kind company is not a hardship. *J'ai beaucoup de chance, non?*" He rose from his chair with a bow that included them all. "*Merci bien.*"

"Not at all," Darcy responded. "It *is* Christmas, when—as our local clergy reminds us—strangers are to be particularly welcomed. I warn you though,

Pemberley will soon be in a whirl of preparation. Likely, it will start today!"

He paused at the door. "You must excuse me. I have some affairs to attend to this morning."

"Bingley," he called, "have you thoughts how we might entertain the Comte?"

"If the pond is cleared, we might go skating. Georgiana, what do you think?"

"If it is not too windy," she replied, her self-possession now steady. *Some vigorous exercise would be just the thing...clear away this unwanted fog.* "I will send for any available boys to clear it again. They will be glad of it for their own games later."

"Unless there is more snow," Bingley reminded them all with a smirk, "but I repeat myself!"

"Some pennies might be very welcome." Georgiana suggested, a pert smile and arched brows aimed at him.

"I shall consult my purse," laughed Bingley. "Bastien, does skating intrigue you?"

~~&~~

Harry was already in the book room when Darcy entered. Standing, hat in hand, his driver pulled on his forelock as Darcy sat down at the desk. "Mr. Darcy, sir."

"Harry, first let me apologize for sending you out in this and at such an hour." He gestured out the window. "I assure you that it was quite urgent, else I would not."

He withdrew Harry's note from his pocket and indicated its contents. "Bad, was it?"

"Wors 'un I've seen in a decade or more, sir. Bless me, but it's more'un I can believe why they didn't put up at Green Man."

"What did you learn?"

"They were lookin' fer Pemberley, sir. Didn't know they were only five miles away nor where to turn off the high road. They were all fair frozen yet left as quick as may be," he added. "Caused quite a stir...*quite* a stir."

"I suppose the mere fact that he was French would—"

"French, sir? No'un said naught 'bout 'em bein' Frenchies!"

Darcy stared at him, concern now changing into something like alarm. "You are sure?"

'You know how Garston feels about Frenchies, 'specially since word of their John dyin' in Portugal. He'd 'ave said somethin'...the usual mob at Green Man would sure 'ave said."

Darcy nodded. "What else?"

"There's a question 'bout a hammer, sir. Those ostler boys come in after the coach left all agog 'bout a hammer. Seems the driver asked for one to fix a problem with the coach. He weren't happy 'til they brought out the biggest one-hand hammer they 'ad."

"The coach had some damage *before* they arrived?"

"So the driver said." Harry shrugged. "Could 'ave been, but no'un saw it. Too dark and more'un too cold to lollygag."

"You said he asked for a hammer," Darcy reminded him.

"W-e-l-l," Harry drew out the word, "the boys say he ne'er returned it. Wanted Garston to know so they'd no be blamed fer loosin' it or mislayin' it somewhere."

"Hmm." Darcy sat back in his chair, chin in hand. After a moment of reverie, he looked up. "Harry, I have more for you. Take Taylor and go over every inch of the coach's undercarriage, the frame, shaft, wheels, the harnessing." He ticked off his list. "And examine the horses. Tell no one, but come up to the house when you are done."

"Sir?"

"I want to know everything you can tell me about this accident."

Chapter 7

Taking her leave of her brother-in-law and the disconcerting presence of the Comte, Georgiana quickly ascended the stairs. The refuge of her rooms was everything she desired, but a diminutive cry from further down the upstairs hall caused her to turn from her door. Hurrying down the expanse of Axminister carpet and around the corner to the Darcy rooms, she knocked quietly. The door opened almost immediately.

"Miss Georgiana!" Annie Fletcher curtsied and, with a question clearly writ on her face, looked back into the room.

"Oh, do let her in!"

"Of course, ma'am," Annie turned back to Georgiana. "The young master is in high dudgeon this morning," she confided with a wry smile and moved aside the entrance.

With an answering quirk of her lips, Georgiana stepped inside to see her sister-in-law still in bed. Usually so collected and ready to be amused with anything life sent her, Elizabeth looked up at her this morning with a mixture of tired frustration and relief.

"Georgiana, my dear, it's so good of you to come!" Little Alexander lay crying lustily in her arms, his swaddling and the bed linens all about in disarray.

"Annie, bring over a chair for Georgie. Yes, close...there." She reached over to pat the seat and, looking up at her hopefully asked, "Would you like to...?" She stopped and closed her eyes. Leaning over, she bestowed a kiss on the baby's forehead. "Of course, you would not! We have all had our turn with him, but Alexander is not best pleased at the moment, are you, my son?"

Georgiana bent close to appraise her nephew's mood. It did not look promising. *And what do you know about babies?* She resolutely held out her arms. "Yes, give him to me." She lifted him, squirming, from Elizabeth and gingerly sat down. The movements gave the child pause and his deep eyes looked up searchingly into her face.

"Oh!" she exclaimed, "He looks...does he not look just like Fitzwilliam?"

"In what way? How do you see it?"

"His colouring, of course; but his eyes...the way he just looked at me. Solemnly, as if he *knows* me... loves me." She glanced at Elizabeth, a blush highlighting her cheeks. "I am being foolish."

"No, no you are not! I have seen the same. It is uncanny." Lizzy sighed and relaxed against the pillows. Immediately, Alexander broke into a wail.

"And now he strongly puts me in mind of another child with which I have intimate experience," she stated with conviction. "My sister Lydia."

Trying not to laugh, Georgiana switched Alexander to her shoulder and began patting his back. "You remember her as a baby?"

"Baby, child, girl, young woman—"

"Lizzy!"

"—and in every missive, I receive from her to this day!"

"That is too much!" Georgiana protested even as she giggled. "Is she not near my age?"

Lizzy drew back and surveyed her sister-in-law with new eyes. "Yes, she is; I had not thought! You seem older, certainly wiser, than 'poor Lydia' as she has become to all in my family."

Reminded by the summary of Lydia's situation, Georgiana sobered. "I cannot but pity your sister, committed, as she is, into the power of such a person as her husband!"

"Oh, Georgie," Lizzy cried, "I should not—"

"Look, he's asleep!" Georgiana interrupted her apology with a whisper. They both scanned the little face, now relaxed in cherubic lines. Annie pulled the bell for Nurse and, upon her arrival, Georgiana carefully lay him in her arms. Both nurse and lady's maid left them, closing the door softly.

Georgiana rose. "You must wish to dress…"

"Annie will return in a few minutes. Before she does…I hope I have not overset you. My wretched tongue runs away with me at times, especially when I mean to be witty. I would not cause you pain for the world!"

"No, it is I who must apologize, having promised myself not to behave in so ungenerous a fashion that you feel you may not speak of your own sister," Georgiana countered. "I am not upset; I promise you. Just sobered by the reminder of what might have been my own fate. Oh, let me help you!" She went to the bedside while Elizabeth finished pulling away the twisted bed linens. "Take my arm."

Once on her feet, Lizzy embraced her. "You know your brother would never have abandoned you, do you not?"

"I know," she whispered. "I wish you had come to know Mrs. Annesley better. You would not be fearful for me."

"She was a godsend," Lizzy ventured.

"Yes, exactly that. Her gentle ways and trust in Providence opened a way for me. She was a clergyman's widow, you know." Lizzy nodded. "We read and studied together, walked—over all Pemberley, I think!—and talked and talked. I shall always honour and love her for that and for leaving me with the means to face life after...what happened, what I almost..." She ceased speaking for a moment, then gave herself an unconscious little shake and continued. "She lives with one of her sons now who has just received his ordination. He is unmarried and needed her help setting up his parish duties."

Elizabeth embraced her again. "And you have been her dedicated pupil, almost a daughter." She paused, then resolved to plunge ahead. "But I think that something is challenging your complacency."

A shadow of dismay shaded Georgiana's countenance. "I have betrayed myself?"

"A strong word for what I think is likely a temporary infatuation with a very handsome stranger." She smiled understandingly. "The Comte is quite charming, his manner meant to please. A young woman would be made of stone if she did not respond to his address in, well, confusing ways?" She waited for Georgiana's response.

"Confusing, yes! And at times, frightening," Georgiana confessed.

"Does he remind you of Wickham?"

"Oh, no, not in any way!" she denied. "It is my own feelings that are reminiscent of what they were then."

"You do not trust yourself, then." Lizzy's brows furrowed.

"I do not understand these feelings; I can hardly name them!" she cried.

A shout from outside the window, drew Elizabeth's attention, giving her a moment to think. Seeing it was a troop of boys with shovels making for the pond, she smiled and turned back to her sister-in-law.

"You are right not to trust your feelings at this time, Georgie. It is much too soon to attribute them to anything more than an appreciation for a young man's beauty and his pleasing attention. *That* is natural and, in a way, common to a man, as well. So do not berate yourself!" She paused, reaching into her own experience for some guidance to give her.

"Enjoy his gallantry," she counselled, "but lightly. Allow enough time to become a little used to the charms he displays. When you do, assuming he is even at

Pemberley that long, you will find the 'misunderstanding' will clear and you will understand your heart."

"Oh, Lizzy, thank you! " Georgiana's face lightened in relief. "You are so wise. It is no wonder that Fitzwilliam loves you!"

"Well, I do not know about wise!" she laughed. "I wish someone had lent me this advice *before* I met your brother. I have learned not to be hasty as I was then, and a little less given to admiration of my own wit. I thank God that when I had the good fortune to get 'used to' him, and our misunderstanding had cleared, your brother offered me a second chance to know my heart."

A knock at the door signalled that Annie was come with Elizabeth's morning attire.

"The day begins!" sighed Lizzy. "Enter," she called, then looked back to Georgiana. "What shall we do with Bastien today?"

"Charles suggested a skating party."

"So, that is why the boys are out clearing the pond so early. Have you heard anything about the roads?"

"They are impassable for miles in every direction."

"We shall have the Comte for some time, I think. Enjoy...but lightly!" Lizzy reminded her as Georgiana turned to leave. "And guard your heart."

"Yes, ma'am," Georgiana replied with a joyful curtsey and whisked out the door.

~~&~~

When he saw that it was Elizabeth at the door, Darcy rose from his desk and met her before she had traversed half the room. Drawing her into an embrace he was quite eager to explore, he lifted her chin for a lingering kiss. "He is asleep, then?" he murmured. To her affirmative, he bent for another. "And we are alone."

"Mmm," she responded, "in the book room."

"Yes... well," he chuckled softly. Tucking her head against his chest, he placed the next kiss on the top of it. "You are a welcome distraction no matter the room..." Another kiss. "...and anytime we find ourselves alone these days I am determined *not* to squander it."

"You *are* the master of Pemberley—

"Let no one forget."

Elizabeth laughed but then pushed away from him just enough to see his face. "Georgiana visited me this morning. We talked. I believe she left in a better frame of mind. Did something happen at breakfast?"

"She was quiet; not unusual when a stranger is present. Why?"

"She was all disordered...as she was last night. I suggested that it was merely a natural response, but one over which she should exercise care. She seemed relieved."

"A 'virtuous wife...her worth is far above rubies!'" he quoted. "'The heart of her husband safely trusts her.'" He pulled her tight for a moment and then released her. "I tell you, though, I am not satisfied with the Comte's account of the circumstances of his arrival and am taking steps." He went back to his desk. "I have written Dy."

"Lord Brougham? London gossip," she replied, her tone dubious.

Darcy hesitated. Should he...? No, he may trust her implicitly, but Dy had not given him leave. "Gossip? You might call it that. Highly placed gossip, you may be sure." And lowly placed as well, he added to himself and resumed his seat. She need not know about Dy yet, especially now with Alexander.

Chapter 8

*O*ur spoons were now ready, and gathering round the pot we dipped them in, not, however, without sundry scalded fingers. Ernest then drew from his pocket the large shell he had procured for his own use, and scooping up a good quantity of soup he put it down to cool, smiling at his own foresight.

"Prudence should be exercised for others," I remarked; "your cool soup will do capitally for the dogs, my boy; take it to them, and then come and eat like the rest of us."

Ernest winced at this, but silently taking up his shell he placed it on the ground before the hungry dogs, who lapped up its contents in a moment...

--*The Swiss Family Robinson*

Georgiana looked up from her book at the knock upon her door. "Yes?" A maid-of-all-work opened her door and curtsied.

"Excuse me, Miss, but Mr. Bingley has sent up to tell you that the pond is cleared should you still wish to skate."

"Thank you, Ellen. Please tell Mr. Bingley I shall be down directly I change."

"Yes, Miss." Ellen curtsied again and closed the door.

With a finger between the pages to keep her place, Georgiana rose and pulled the bell for her lady's maid. Book still in hand, she went to her window where she could only just see the pond's edge. It had taken most of the morning, but it was clear of snow and the boys had even shovelled a crooked little path out to it.

They have surely earned their pennies!

In fewer than five minutes, Barrow emerged from the dressing room door. "Is it a skating party, Miss Darcy? It's that cold on the pond, Miss."

"There *will be* a fire, Barrow, but you are right. As warm as you can bundle me but still move, please." She looked down at her book, slipped in a piece of lace, and laid it aside with some reluctance. Fitzwilliam had presented it to her when last he'd returned from London. "On a recommendation," he had said. She had to agree. *It was quite good!*

Barrow returned with her arms full of clothing. In short order, Georgiana chose from among her warmest gowns and motioned toward the new pelisse of dark green wool she had worn on the journey home from London. A matching hood lined in soft white rabbit's fur and a fur muff completed her ensemble. Pausing to drop a small purse of pennies into a pocket, should Bingley forget, she then hurried out her door and down the stairs.

Her brother-in-law awaited her at the bottom and offered his arm down the icy steps and courtyard. "You look splendid, Georgiana!"

"Why, thank you," she replied with pleasure. *Charles is always attentive to such things. Was it his sisters or his gentle wife that had taught him so?*

"Bastien is already at the pond and has set the fire to blaze so we will not freeze. I wish Jane could join us," he continued in a wistful voice, "but that is, of course, impossible."

"Just two more months!" she reminded him.

"Two more," he affirmed with a nodded. Then his habitual smile turned down. "But will I be ready, do you think? I am the youngest in my family. No little brothers or sisters, no babies in the house while growing up."

Georgiana blinked up at him, as much in dismay how to reply as at the sharpness of the air.

He glanced down at her as they assayed the boys' irregular path, a crooked grin now gaining ground upon his face. "Therefore, as in everything, your brother must be my model."

"You could not have a better," she replied and squeezed his arm.

They were now in sight of the pond and could see the Comte crouched at the fire. He rose and waved at their approach, then dusted snow from the bench nearby.

"*Bonjour*, again, *Mademoiselle*. Bingley and myself have already a fire. Will you sit?"

"*Merci*," she replied, taking his extended hand to steady her as she sat down. She deliberately offered him a small, quick smile to show him that she *was* capable of disinterested courtesy in his presence.

"Allow me." Bingley knelt gingerly in the snow and strapped the skates onto her stout boots. The Comte had retreated to the ice while he did so, executing strong but graceful arcs upon the glistening ice. Georgiana could not help but attend to his ease and fearlessness on such an uncertain stage. *He is no more concerned than if he were merely crossing a ballroom floor.*

When she stood to descend the shallow bank, he quickly returned to its edge. "*Vous me permettez.*" He extended his hand again. "Allow me. It may be *dangereux*...a little." His smile was open, yet because she could be its only object, she felt a quiver in her breast that had nothing to do with the cold.

Before she could think, she reached out to him. His grip closed firmly upon her hand, and he led her out onto the ice.

He did not release her immediately, but held her hand lightly until she found her balance. When she did, he let it go. Then, pushing off with powerful strokes ahead of her, he surprised her by turning around to continue backward, sending her a challenging laugh. Her heart rising to match his exuberance at the freedom and speed the ice offered, she struck out as well.

As the bank flew past her, Georgiana revelled in the smoothness of the ice. *Had it ever been so, even in her girlhood when she had chased Fitzwilliam across this frozen expanse?* She met the cold with a grin at the memory when, at five years of age, she had begged their father for skates. Father had called Fitzwilliam into the book room that Christmas and assigned him the task as she had stood next to the desk, trembling in hopeful excitement.

Sixteen at the time, Fitzwilliam had not looked overjoyed with the prospect, but in deference to their father's wishes, he had taken her out as soon as the blacksmith had fashioned skates of the proper size. The lightness in her heart increased, remembering how he had taught and teased her over the ice, laughing at her shrieks of determination to catch him. There had been falls and bruises, of course; but with his encouragement and vast quantities of Cook's hot chocolate, she had learnt.

Suddenly, Charles flashed past her with a whoop. Sending fond memories back to the past, she doubled her effort. Ahead of her, Charles had drawn even with the Comte and a contest had ensued. *But where is the finishing line?* She laughed to herself at this peculiarity of the male race that could make anything a competition. Looking away to the snow-filled meadow and park beyond, she filled her lungs with the crisp, winter air. *Glorious! What a blessing that Charles had suggested skating*!

Although she had increased her speed, Charles and the Comte were soon close behind her. In seconds they were past, Charles's arms up in a declaration of victory.

Oh, she laughed, *I was the finish!* Both of them came to a stop, breathing heavily, and waited for her to catch up. As she drew near, Charles turned and pushed off again, but the Comte continued to wait. She slowed as she neared him. *Should I stop or pass him by?*

The Comte solved her dilemma by again extending his hand. The illusion of a dance floor was so strong that she withdrew a hand from her muff and offered it without thought. Grasping it lightly, he turned her off into the centre of the pond with ease, then pulled it into the crook of his arm before she knew what to do.

"*Mademoiselle* Darcy, you skate well," he murmured. "*Mais bien sûr*, you have this pond, *c'est magnifique*, always at your disposal. Did you learn as a child?"

"My...my brother taught me." His closeness was disconcerting...but also exciting. "*Encourage a new acquaintance to speak about themselves,*" Mrs. Annesley's directive came to her rescue. Before she could form a question to that end, the Count, still in possession of her hand, released her to arm's length and swung before her, skating backward.

"Ah, now I can see you! *Beaucoup mieux!*" The delight on his face made her laugh. "Did your brother teach you to dance?"

"On skates?"

"*Oui, Mademoiselle,* on skates, on the ice."

Georgiana looked at him doubtfully.

"You do not believe?" He swung back to her side. "I will teach you. Count! *Un, deux, trois, quatre*, then we come close. Count again and we skate away but do not let go! *Commencer!*"

"One, two, three, four!" She leaned toward him. The space closed between them.

"*Un, deux, trois, quatre.*" They parted to arm's length.

"*De nouveau!*"

"One, two, three, four," Georgiana repeated and returned close to his side.

"*Excellent*" he commended her. "And now, present to me your other hand. Yes, you must push away the so charming muff. *Merci*." He possessed the hand that emerged from the white fur, pulling it and the muff across her waist and dropped the other. His free arm suddenly encircled her waist and she found herself pulled up against his side.

"Count to eight," he prompted *Un, deux, trois...*"

What should I do? She could feel her panic rising.

"*...sic, sept, huit.*" His counting out of the beats distracted her. She could not decide. "Now, we shall switch back our hands at length." In a moment, he released her, drifting from her side and reaching for her other hand. He slowed to a stop. "It is like a dance, no?"

A dance? She calmed with the thought. *Nothing more than a dance...enjoy him, but lightly.*

"Yes, it is!" she answered him.

"And would you like to practice this new way to dance?"

"What are you two doing?" Bingley called, circling them and coming to a stop. "I say, Bastien, you almost looked to be dancing!"

"*Nous étions, mon ami,*" Bastien replied. "We were! We were dancing on the ice!" His brows rose in question to her. "Shall we show this *incroyant*, this unbeliever?"

"You'll catch cold if you just stand about," Bingley urged, circling them again.

"All the more reason," Bastien held out his hand. "*Mademoiselle* Darcy, may I have this dance?"

"You may, sir." Somehow, she accomplished a shallow curtsey on the ice.

"Bastien," he requested her. "*S'il vous plaî.* I am so very far from friends."

Georgiana hesitated, surprised at this request, for it was not quite proper. But the hopeful look he cast her, his stranded circumstances, and the thought of Christmas without family or friends melted all her reserve. "*Oui...*Bastien," she agreed, "but only on the ice."

"*C'est suffisant.* It is enough." His bright blue eyes shone with pleasure. "Shall we?"

Georgiana took her place next to him, arm outstretched, as the warmth of his regard enveloped her. "*Un, deux, trois, quatre...*"

~~&~~

It was mid-evening and already the moon was valiantly pressing forward against advancing clouds that would be heavy, his steward predicted, with snow. Darcy looked away from the fierce engagement outside his book room window and back into the faces of Harry and Taylor, his driver and stablemaster.

"You are sure?"

"Yes, sir," they both replied.

His jaw clenched in a grim line, Darcy dismissed them, with thanks, to their dinners and repeated his caution to keep everything to themselves. With a pull of their forelocks, they left and Darcy turned again to the struggle beyond his window. *More snow!* He devoutly hoped not! Especially not with what he had just learned.

"No hammer has been found in the coach," they had declared. "Probably thrown away after it was used." And used, it had been! Neither Harry nor Taylor could *swear* that it was the cause of all the damage on the undercarriage and wheels, but the smashed wood at critical points argued in its favour. How the coach had been tipped over, neither man could guess. Some of the driving lines appeared to have snapped or possibly been cut "most ways through a 'fore hand"—it was hard to say—and the shaft was cracked and useless.

The horses appeared to be unscathed, which Harry called a "miracle" unless the accident had been a sham. Neither was there a sign that any of them had suffered lately from a stone caught in a hoof. Taylor assured him that some repairs and replacements could be made from Pemberley's stores, but no one on the estate was a coachmaker. It would be a patched-up affair at best. "Better they got to Chesterfield for that, if it's north they're going, but no farther," had been their considered judgment. "And it will take some time to do what we can here."

"The Comte's driver and valet, what of them?"

The driver, they reported as a taciturn sort, keeping to himself and shrugging off any attempts to engage him. The stable lads were leery of his curses if they happened near the Comte's horses and studiously avoided them and his company. The valet, they knew nothing about, as he took his meals in the house.

So, there it is! His caution had been justified, his suspicions nearly so. *Why here?* he asked himself. The next question followed hard upon the first: *Could it be that Georgiana is his object?* It seemed fantastical given the planning and expense involved. *To hazard all on such an uncertain outcome? Why not pay less costly court to her in London?* A flake of snow drifted past his window, then several more, and Darcy wondered, as he searched for a glimpse of the undaunted sliver of moon, how far his letter to Dy had travelled that day.

~~&~~

Save for the guttering of a candle, the scratching of her pen upon the page of her journal was all that disturbed the silence in Georgiana's rooms. It was late. Barrow had already prepared her for bed, so she wrote at leisure, seated at her elegantly carved escritoire, without fear of interruption...or discovery.

It was shortly after her arrival at Pemberley that Mrs. Annesley had suggested she begin a journal. "I have kept one for years," she had confided to the sad, listless girl, "and find it helps to order my thoughts. The discipline of recording your prayers, naming your fears, asking your questions and keeping the answers will encourage you—a testament to the work in your life of a loving Providence, my dear. I promise!"

Doubtful of such a hopeful result, she had obediently joined her new companion in daily journal keeping.

Single sentences for the day eventually became a paragraph, paragraphs then became pages. As they wrote together, walked and talked together, her trust in the future returned and her melancholy faded.

Faithfulness to her journal faltered with Mrs. Annesley's departure. Then, just when the heady whirl of her first Season threatened to overwhelm her, Mrs. Annesley's place had been taken up by another whose understanding she had come to trust implicitly. At first, her replacement had been surprising, but had not Fitzwilliam himself, and more than once, put her in his care?

No matter that her entries were seen by no one but herself. It was enough that he was waiting for her, there on paper, and today she had so much to tell him...about Bastien.

December 16, 1813
Dear Lord Brougham...

Chapter 9

Friday, December 17, 1813

As is often the case after a winter's storm, the next morning dawned clear and achingly bright. The reflection of the sun from a brilliantly blue sky upon the new layer of snow threw reflections of such brightness into the breakfast room as had not been seen in anyone's recent memory. The well-polished wood of the table gleamed, the silver sparkled, even the gilt frames of the paintings upon the wall glowed.

"It is a wonder," Bingley addressed them as they sat at breakfast, "that even the subjects of your paintings are not forced to shade their eyes, it is so bright!" Plate in hand, he looked down the table and deliberately took a seat with his back to the windows that lined the room.

Although Darcy had been polite but distant since the Comte had joined them in the breakfast room, he had to laugh with the others at Bingley's witticism. He then motioned to a portrait above the sideboard. "Charles, I believe you are right! The Duke of Marlborough just blinked for the first time in 150 years!"

"On a more serious note, Darcy," Bingley began when the laughter had died down, "has anyone reached Lambton or even your front gate?"

The question sobered Darcy immediately. "No, a lane had almost reached the gate when last night's snow struck. You might approach it on horseback, but certainly not yet in a carriage. Neither the road to Lambton, which has not been cleared at all. By horse, it would be possible, but very slow going."

"Is it always this way, with the snow?" Bastien asked, looking round the table. "Perhaps my father's choice of a new home is not wise?"

"Not at all," Georgiana hurried to disabuse his notion. "We do have snow almost every year at Christmas and throughout the winter, just not so much or so often. It is beautiful, though, you must admit!"

Glancing at her over his cup, Darcy noted that the smile she cast the Comte, no less than her speech, held far less than her wonted degree of shyness. His heart faltered a beat.

The others all turned in their chairs to look out the windows to behold a scene worthy to be painted.

"*Oui, Mademoiselle, de grande beauté.* It is very beautiful."

Darcy looked back to his sister in time to observe a warm flush suffuse her cheeks. Quickly, he shifted his gaze to the Comte but was met only with a disarming smile directed down the table at him. Silence reigned as they all addressed their breakfasts and the servants entered to refill cups of tea or coffee. A new plate of pastries was presented to each of them in turn and then laid upon the table.

"Even so, it is now seven days until Christmas Eve," Bingley reminded them. "What needs be done that can be done?"

"Yes, how do you observe *le Noël* in this part of England? Is it very different?" Bastien asked.

"I am still learning, myself," Bingley laughed. "This will be my first Christmas in the countryside of Derbyshire."

"You are not from Derbyshire, Charles?"

"Scarborough. In Yorkshire, but on the coast. We have a townhouse there in the city. My sisters will spend their Christmas there, although they had hoped for an invitation to Pemberley. But, customs in the country and at large estates can be quite different." He looked to Darcy for confirmation. "And every village has its own, I think."

"We are not so exotic, Charles," Darcy replied, "and this year at Pemberley, particularly so."

"We are not hosting the county as we usually do for Christmas," Georgiana responded to Bastien's questioning look. "Most Christmases we entertain not only our tenants but also the villagers in Lambton as well as our friends from other great houses in the area. The work is prodigious, but it is all great fun and a way of extending the joy of Christmas and relief for the poor."

"This is marvellous!" exclaimed Bastien. "And this will not be so, why?" He paused and then coloured. "Ah...of course, I forget. Le bébé!"

"A luxury to which we are not privileged," Bingley sighed dramatically, explaining to the bemused Comte.

"Mrs. Bingley attends Mrs. Darcy, you see, and the little fellow is remarkably peckish at night. But, to my original question." He turned to Darcy. "What needs to be done that we may be of help?

"Fitzwilliam, is it not time the holly and ivy were gathered? Perhaps, the tree could be chosen, as well." Georgiana looked in question to her brother.

"Perhaps," Darcy echoed her. "Allow me to question the steward."

"A tree? You follow the German custom?"

"Yes," Darcy answered him quickly before Georgiana could respond, "Our Queen brought it with her as a Christmas tradition and we have observed it here at Pemberley for the past ten years. It is especially loved by children." He grinned at his sister. "I remember one such child who enjoyed it *very* much and would hardly stay asleep long enough for it to be decorated."

"Georgiana! Surely, not you?" Bingley teased.

Georgiana blushed but rallied to the account. "Of course! What child could resist the silver paper, toys, and candied fruit? It was magical! And my brother was not so old that he did not enjoy chasing me back to bed."

"Delightful," murmured the Comte, his eyes warm upon her.

This time, it was not a falter of his heart that Darcy felt, but a decided twist. *The fellow was making love to her at his own breakfast table!*

"I say, I would favour some exercise this morning, if you do not mind, Darcy." Bingley set aside his napkin and pushed back his chair. "I propose a short expedition on horseback as far as your gate. Upon our return, you will have had word from your steward whether a sled can pierce your park for a holly hunt. What do you say?" he asked them all.

"*Excellent!*" Bastien supported the notion with a clap of his hands. "*Mademoiselle*, you will go, also?"

"It sounds a wonderful idea!" Georgiana agreed in answer to the Comte, pleasure suffusing her face. "Yes, I will join you!"

"Perhaps I will join you, also," Darcy quickly interjected. It was not what he had planned for this morning. He considered his sister, her face aglow as they spoke of the projected outing. Elizabeth had told Georgiana to "enjoy" the Comte's attentions, and yesterday he had been mollified, but this morning! To his way of thinking, she was *enjoying* him far too much! And the Comte...*too interested by half*!

"I'll direct the horses be ready for us at one." He rose. "If you will excuse me, I have matters upon which to attend. Georgiana, any letters?"

"Soon, if the servant may wait an hour?"

"As you wish," Darcy nodded and then turned to the Comte. "I will gladly frank any letters you may have, as well. You must wish to allay the concern of those expecting you. How quickly they may arrive at their destinations is another matter. We have had no word of the roads in any direction from Lambton, although we may hope that roads south of Derbyshire are in better condition. North, to the countryside around York, will be difficult."

The Comte seemed to hesitate.

"You will find all you need in the library desk. Please, consider it at your disposal."

"You are most kind, sir," the Comte bowed.

"Not at all," Darcy returned the bow and with a quick glance at his sister, left the room.

~~~&~~~

"Here is your papa, Alexander. Just in time!" Elizabeth was already dressed and clearly awaiting him when Darcy entered their rooms from breakfast. He did not have more than a moment to briefly wonder what he was "in time" for when his heir was pushed into his arms with a sigh from his mama.

"Annie has yet to dress my hair." Only then did Darcy note that her hair still fell in luxuriant, auburn waves down her back. "But Alexander would rather be taken for a walk by his mama. Nurse would not do, you understand." She smoothed the swaddling blanket from the baby's face and tucked it in a corner. "Perhaps, papa will?" she cooed, and gave him a gentle chuck under his chin that was answered with the sunniest of smiles.

Darcy laughed, "Charming the ladies already, are we?" Alexander's little brow furrowed at the loud sound. "Now, now," his father whispered, "none of that." He looked to Elizabeth, who had taken her seat at the dressing table. "What now?"

"Walk on, sir!"

"Ahh, a tour of the estate..." He looked down and was caught as before by curiously alert little eyes.

"The room is sufficient, my dear husband," she chuckled as Annie Fletcher took a comb to her tangle of tresses.

Darcy ran a finger lightly over his son's cheek. "Off we go, then." *What would amuse an infant?* He walked slowly to the sunlit window.

"What is the news of the world? Did anything interesting arise at breakfast beside talk of the weather?"

"Several things, but by their absence," Darcy replied, shifting Alexander to face the window. "The Comte seems not to take much interest in the condition of his coach or the repairs it will need. He has not inquired about them once nor summoned his driver to discuss them."

"Would that be odd for a scion of the *Ancien Régime*?"

"Perhaps not," he agreed. "He also had to be reminded to write to his father and whoever he is to meet in York about the estate he is to purchase. It is more than curious! He was in such a fever to get there that he forced his servants and horses into a storm, yet he is not anxious to inform anyone of his delay."

A whimper arose from the bundle of swaddling. Darcy turned from the window. "Lost its charm already, has it?" he addressed the bundle.

"I think it is the movement he likes, rather than the view," his wife observed.

"He is certainly 'viewing' *me* quite intently!" He looked back down. "I can almost believe he is peering right into...into my soul." Darcy shook his head. "Such strange thoughts!"

"Not so strange," Elizabeth replied softly.

Another whimper reminded Darcy to resume his perambulation. "Yes, agreed. This is not a time for philosophy. It is movement that is wanted and Papa, it seems, is your horse to command." He set off to the other side of the room. "That reminds me, we are going to take some exercise later on horseback with a short expedition to the Lambton Road gate. Then, Georgiana is keen to look for holly and choose the yew for Christmas. I wish you could accompany us."

"Can that be done? It seems a bit early." Elizabeth patted a few last curls into place as Annie stepped back from her labour. She rose to watch her husband continue about the room.

"The ride to the gate is possible. The rest probably will have to be postponed for a few days." He waited until Annie curtsied and closed the dressing room door behind her. "Have you thought about how we may occupy the Comte? I have sent him to write his letters *alone* in the library and we ride at one, but Georgiana is to come as well."

"Georgiana?" Her brow lowered in perplexity. "Why— Oh, you wish to occupy him with something *other* than Georgiana? You still foresee a problem?"

Darcy turned and, biting his lip, regarded her steadily. "Even if the circumstances of his arrival were not troubling, the swift nature of their attraction to each other is certainly so. I can see it in Georgiana's face and manner. And the Comte!"

She cocked her head at him. "It is hardly to be wondered at, Fitzwilliam! They are the only two young people at Pemberley. She is beautiful as well as young, with a compassionate nature. He is handsome, self-effacing...with a little of the lost lamb about him."

"And he dresses well. Yes, I know," Darcy responded drily, recalling their last conversation.

Elizabeth shook her head at him, a wry smile upon her lips. "Georgiana is more aware of herself than you may think. She is not the same innocent as before, nor is she alone and at the mercy of a scheming governess." She lay an assuring hand on his arm. "She is well surrounded by people who love her...the best place to explore her heart if we will allow her."

The deep breath her husband took at her words, and the crinkle of his brow, told Elizabeth that she had been heard, but that he still was not at peace. "But she is your sister, and it is hard to see her changing into a young woman." She patted his arm. "So it will be with this little one as he grows into a young man." She looked down into their child's face.

"Oh, look!" she whispered suddenly, "He is asleep!"

"What now?" Darcy whispered back.

"We ring for Nurse."

Chapter 10

Clad in a smart riding ensemble of deep blue wool trimmed in velvet of the same shade, Georgiana skipped down the stairs to meet with the others for the riding party. She was early and eager for the expedition. Like her brother, she was an accomplished rider and therefore could not deny that she was curious what the Comte's bearing might be astride a pure-blood horse from Pemberley's well-known stables.

Seeing no one yet in in the hall, she set her hat on a table and wandered down a side hall toward the library where she was met by a footman.

"Miss Darcy," he stopped and bowed. "There is a problem in the library."

"The library?"

"It's Master Trafalgar, Miss."

A series of sharp barks sent them both hurrying to the door which lay open to the hall.

"Thank God, you've returned!" a voice came to them from within as the footman entered the room ahead of her. He stepped aside and Georgiana entered the library to see the Comte held in a corner by a triumphant Trafalgar.

"Oh, my goodness!" Georgiana exclaimed in embarrassment both for Bastien and the behavior of her brother's mischievous dog. "Trafalgar, come here, naughty boy!" But the 'naughty boy' was too well acquainted with those terms to be deterred from his prize. Instead, he loosed a low but meaningful growl at this one who was obviously an intruder.

"He will not bite you," Georgiana assured the Comte.

Bastien looked at her doubtfully but attempted to side-step the animal. This was countered with another growl. "*Mademoiselle*, I think you may be wrong. He does not like me."

"Oh, what is the command for release?" She looked to the footman for help but he could only shrug. "I so rarely go hunting with Fitzwilliam..." She looked about the library, trying to remember and shaking her head in frustration.

"*Mademoiselle,* your...your brother perhaps?" Bastien shifted his stance against the bookshelves, his every move followed by the hound. Another growl, culminating with a bark, warned him to remain where he was.

Then, "Ah yes, that's it!"

"*Leicht! Leicht,* Trafalgar," she commanded in German and clicked her tongue.

The look of disappointment on the hound's face was plain. The delightful game was, apparently, at an end and the intruder was to be accepted. Obediently, he backed one step away from his quarry and sat, every muscle perfectly still, but the look in his eyes spoke clearly to those who knew him—*accepted but still suspicious.*

"I am so sorry, Bastien!" Georgiana apologized, "Trafalgar is Fitzwilliam's hunter but also a companion, so he is often about the house." She advanced to the waiting animal and dropped down next to him, ruffling him between the ears. He turned his head and gave her hand a quick lick.

Bastien eased out of the corner and gave them a wide berth.

Georgiana rose. "My brother often calls him 'Monster.' He can be quite mischievous, as you have seen."

"*Monstre! Oui,* that I can believe." Bastien and the dog continued to eye each other as the Comte drifted backward toward the library door. "But 'Trafalgar'? It is a naval battle of some years ago, no?

"Yes, eight years ago." Darcy answered from behind him, surveying the scene from the library door with a quizzical eye. Trafalgar broke his pose at the sound and, trotting over to Darcy's side, sat down with the aplomb of a job well done.

"My brother is a great admirer of Admiral Lord Nelson," Georgiana explained. "In a few moments, you will meet his favourite horse—"

"Nelson," Darcy finished for her, adding "who is not accustomed to being kept waiting once he is saddled in the best of weather. Are you ready, Bastien? The horses have been brought up from the stables."

"I need only my hat and gloves on the hall table."

"Excellent! Charles is awaiting us." He placed his own hat upon his dark locks." Monster?" he addressed the hound at his feet and both pivoted to the hall.

"Will he accompany us?" Bastien whispered to Georgiana as they walked to the hall.

"Oh, yes. Traf always goes with us when my brother or I ride over our lands."

"There you are!" Bingley greeted them when they'd gained the entrance hall. "It's sharpish out there, but we shall warm up soon, I've no doubt."

The Comte's smile was distracted as he donned his hat and gloves, but brightened when he observed Georgiana take her riding hat to a mirror and pin it into place. The footman who had brought her to the library bent, and taking up the train of her skirt, laid it over her arm.

"*Ravissant!*" he declared her, bending down with a voice pitched low for her ears alone. "*Permettez-moi.*" He offered his arm and whispered, "The stairs, they will be dangerous." Amused and delighted with his gallantry, Georgiana accepted his arm and the Comte swept them past her unsmiling brother into the bright afternoon.

~~~&~~~

The riders picked their way across the icy cobblestones of the yard, through the echoing confines of the arch, and gained the drive that wound its way a mile and more to the Lambton gate. The horses were eager to work off the days of confinement in the stable and Darcy, in particular, was occupied reining in Nelson's fire and determination to be in the lead.

"I fear that they all need a good run before we shall get any peace," Darcy called back to the rest of the party just as Nelson flung out a rear hoof and bumped him up from the saddle. "Here now!" he admonished the big black. "None of that!" Taking a rein, he pulled his head about and faced the group. "Bastien?" he queried narrowly even as Nelson danced with impatience.

"*Ne t'inquiètes pas pour moi*," the Comte answered him. "If this horse is willing, I will match you."

Georgiana cast them both a look of concern. "Fitzwilliam, my Lord Comte—"

"So be it!" Darcy turned Nelson again as the Comte brought his mount up. "To the top of the hill! Huzzah!" he yelled and they were off, Trafalgar streaking joyously apace.

Bingley and Georgiana's horses danced about, anxious for their release into the race, but Georgiana first looked to Charles. "Reckless!" she cried, shaking her head, her eyes wide. Immediately, she saw that he did not entirely agree.

"Catch up when you can!" he called to her. A hearty "Huzzah!" arose, and he was gone.

"Ohhhh!" she howled after them all, beset by trepidation but also by a primal urgency that was unwilling to be left behind. Her bay gelding shivered with excitement and, stamping a hoof, called loudly after the others. Caution abruptly shed its virtue. Gathering her reins, she settled firmly into the saddle. "All right, Lucius! Huzzah!"

As she expected, Lucius bolted with his permission, determined to catch up and win the lead. He was a strong animal, almost as tall as Nelson, but she was entirely up to his weight. Fitzwilliam had long ago encouraged that she become an accomplished horsewoman, largely, she suspected, because she had been so persistent in her girlhood to follow him everywhere, including on horseback. Then, after Father had died, long, hard rides had been his solace. He had eventually accepted her company, but only with the proviso that she must keep up. From that day, a 'lady's mount' had been rejected.

The cleared lane was only adequate for a single horse, so Georgiana contented herself with catching up to her brother-in-law and easing Lucius into a collected canter as they approached the top of the hill and the two who awaited them. Her brother was bent over Nelson's withers, stroking the horse's neck in praise, but Bastien sat erect, hand on hip, with eyes and a smile that were, she knew, for her. Any question of his horsemanship, how he sat a horse, was answered with a shiver that Georgiana knew did not originate in the cold.

She saw Fitzwilliam address the Comte and, after directing a pull of regret on his lips at her, Bastien turned his horse to set out next to him. Disappointed, Georgiana paired with Charles and they continued on to the gate at a walk.

~~~&~~~

"Bastien," Darcy began what he anticipated would be an uncomfortable inquiry, "what do you know of the condition of your coach? Have you spoken to your driver?" There was only the sound of hooves on gravel for some moments.

"*Oui, mon ami*," he sighed, "Grayson has said that much is damaged. Your steward has approached him, yes? He offers repair for many things—*je suis dans votre dette*—but some are beyond skill of your servants and others, some time to complete. I fear," he continued, lowering his eyes, "that I remain your guest for a while longer."

Darcy could not bring himself to utter the usual assurances, choosing instead to offer information that might give the Comte pause. "We will be more in a few days. My uncle and aunt, Lord and Lady Matlock, arrive on Tuesday, St. Thomas' Day, Lord willing that it does not snow heavily again. It would be a great hardship to the poor, especially this winter."

"Why to the poor? What is St. Thomas's Day to the English?"

"It is the tradition that on St. Thomas' Day the poor and elderly are permitted to go about begging without being troubled. It is expected that they will be greeted everywhere with kindness and given provision for Christmas in food or money."

Bingley edged his horse closer. "Bastien, have you never heard the St. Thomas's Day song?"

"Christmas is coming and the geese are getting fat," Georgiana sang out.

"Please spare a penny for the old man's hat," Bingley joined her.

If you haven't got a penny, a ha'penny will do;
If you haven't got a ha'penny, God bless you!

They ended with a shout and laughed together and at the Comte's incredulity.

"So much joy!" He looked at them with wonder. "In Austria, it was a day for exorcising demons. A priest comes with incense and the holy water while we pray the house be cleansed of devils. Among the *émigrés*, we prayed so also for France." He looked away. "Very solemn."

"We bring our gifts to Lambton to distribute and then meet our aunt and uncle at the Green Man for a wassail cup before we all travel together back to Pemberley," Georgiana explained to the Comte. Turning to Fitzwilliam, she queried, "Or is it the Black Mare's Head this year?" But he was not attending to her. Rather, he was studying the Comte. "Brother?" *Why was he looking at Bastien so strangely?*

"The Mare's Head," Darcy replied briefly. "We should pick up our pace." Nelson was glad to oblige and broke into an easy trot at his master's urging. Leaving the others to do likewise, Darcy was alone in the lead for only moments, but it was enough to ponder what might be the reason for Bastien's startled reaction. It was quickly resolved. *Lambton...The Green Man—of course!*

In a quarter hour they reached the Lambton gate. Darcy advanced into the centre of the road and surveyed the drifts along it, north and south. There was evidence of some stragglers on foot, some on horseback, but nothing resembling a sleigh or carriage track had yet been worn into the snow. A cloud of steamy breath rose into the crisp air, signalling his dismay, as the others joined him to see the road for themselves.

"It is four days until St. Thomas's," Charles reminded his subdued companions. "Surely the road will be clear enough by then to travel by sleigh!"

Gathering himself, Darcy attempted a smile at his friend, "Yes, you are right. If it does not snow hard again Pemberley will clear the road to Lambton. All will be well."

A sharp breeze blew up the road, followed by urgent reminders from Trafalgar that tarrying in the cold, snowy road was not the height of wisdom for man nor beast.

"Shall we?" Darcy's invitation was readily accepted and they all turned their horses back down Pemberley's drive. He watched uneasily as, ahead of him, the Comte quickly brought his mount up to Georgiana's. He leaned toward her and, saying something that Darcy could not hear, elicited a burst of happy laughter from her, which he then joined.

Where is that letter? The question remained as insistent and speculative as it had the day before. *If the way to London is clear south of Derbyshire, Dy could have it by tomorrow morning. Then what?* Knowing his friend, there would definitely be something.

Chapter 11

The riders returned and, after a cup of warmed punch had been offered to revive them, dispersed to change from their riding dress. Seeing them off up the stairs, Darcy spun about and inquired of the footman where his wife might be.

"In the Yellow Salon, sir," was the reply. With a nod to the man, he strode to the delicately exquisite room that had been his mother's favourite retreat and had now become his wife's.

At his entrance, Elizabeth looked up from an issue of *La Belle Assemblée*, a wrinkle of concentration still gracing her brow that evolved into one of question at his arrival in the Salon still in his riding attire.

"Yes, pardon me," Darcy acknowledged, "but it could not wait." He sat on the edge of the opposite chair and leaned earnestly toward her. "I beg you, keep Georgiana close by you today. I would have her privately engaged with our guest as little as possible for the remainder of the day."

"What has happened?" Elizabeth laid down the magazine.

"Little things—you would laugh at a recital of them, but together..." his mouth formed a hard line. "Taken together, there is a sense of campaign about them I wish discouraged."

"I imagine you *would* recognize a campaign when you saw one," she commented with an arch look that rarely failed to make him laugh. "I remember a rather successful one launched from these very halls and against *impossible* odds."

"Do you, now?" Darcy rose and held out his hand. "And did you see it as it came upon you?" She placed her hand in his and allowed him to raise her to her feet. "Encompassed you?" He pulled her close.

"Well, not at first. It was very subtle, you know," she responded, looking up at him, her archness melting into something else.

"Almost upon you before you had realized..." he whispered into her hair. She shivered.

"Very like that, yes," she confessed into his shoulder.

Darcy's hand passed lightly down her back, came up it, and outlined her jaw. Then lifting her chin, he lightly brushed her lips with his. "Hmm...Caught!"

Elizabeth's eyes widened as she stared directly into the triumph of his, then narrowed in chagrin. With a push, she attempted to disentangled herself, but it was only when he dropped his arms and stepped back that she stood free.

"Oh! Unfair!" she exclaimed, adding irrationally, "And you smell of horse!"

"Exactly the point I wished to make," he replied quietly, ignoring her jibe. He caught her hand again, this time raising it to his lips. "It is the little things that creep into the heart, softening it into allowing small intimacies that then tempt it to greater ones."

"Or it could be that a personable young man, lonely and bereft of family, who as a child was constantly moved about the world, appears to you too quick to create a longed-for intimacy among strangers," Elizabeth countered sharply, nursing her wounded sensibilities.

Darcy released her hand and shrugged. "You may be right that all is as it appears: an unfortunate accident that seems to be turning into a very fortunate one." He ceased speaking and turning from her, circled the room in thought before coming once again to her side, his face grave. "I have not shared all I have learned with you and will not burden you with concerns that are mine to bear. This I will tell you in my defence: there was no accident. The coach was deliberately wrecked; it is all but certain."

~~~&~~

Georgiana found Elizabeth's invitation just as her maid bent to the ravages the wonderful hour of skating had visited upon her hair. Seated before her dressing table, she saw that her colour was still high when the maid finished and so decided to linger in her chamber before joining the others. Should anyone notice, she could attribute the rose of her cheeks and the liveliness of her eyes to the cold and wind, but it would be wiser to avoid the risk for such a tale would not be the truth.

No, the thrilling flutters of restlessness that had been coursing through her had everything to do with the thrill of 'dancing' with Bastien's arm about her on the frozen pond and a whispered plea for an assignation later in the library. She had known at once that she must reject it. But she had not. Instead, she had faltered at his entreaty and left him in the lower hall with a jumble of words that, from the look upon his face, he had taken as agreement.

Why did you not made an excuse or simply refuse such an improper request? The sensation of the pull of his arm and the warmth of his side as they had circled the pond spread through her, furnishing her the unanswerable truth. Neither of them had wanted the sweet unity of their movements in the dance to end.

Barrow patted the last curl into place and being dismissed, disappeared with a curtsey into the dressing room. It was then that Georgiana's eye was caught by Elizabeth's forgotten missive lying beside her combs. She frowned at it.

What could it be, that Lizzy had not just sent her message via a servant?

Plucking it up, Georgiana unfolded the note and read the short lines. Suddenly, a hot rush of unwonted resentment washed over her, overthrowing all the exhilaration of the last hour spent in the pleasurable company of the attentive and fascinating Comte.

She crumbled the note and, throwing it on the dressing table, rose from the chair with a cry, unable to give a name to what she felt. In so doing, she caught a glimpse of herself in the mirror. Her reflection revealed a shockingly rebellious eye.

Why? she demanded of her reflection. *Why did you not refuse him?* The force of her emotions almost unbalanced her. *Because you are falling in love with him and wished to meet him, come what may!*

Shutting her eyes tightly against the plainspoken exposure of what she had not dared to think, she whirled away from the creature in the mirror. *What will you do now? You cannot go!*

A few moments of tumultuous reflection brought Elizabeth's note back to her mind. Quickly, she retrieved it and reading it once more, the invitation took on the aspect of a command. A way forward unfolded itself.

The note...the summons offers the perfect excuse, even more a justification, for not appearing in the library. Lizzy's claim upon her is the superior, is it not? Bastien would be disappointed, but he cannot fault me!

She breathed an unsteady sigh of relief and composing herself for a time, looked about for her embroidery basket. Retrieving it from near her reading chair, she again looked over into the mirror, examining her reflection again for any tale it might tell.

Nothing there. She tested a smile. *Still nothing...nothing that would raise...questions.* The deceitfulness of her purpose then struck her, arousing unwanted memories. Her smile faded.

But Bastien is nothing like...I do not mean to...

She stared at her glass image and the mask there that she had composed upon her face. It might deceive others, a small voice told her, but it could do naught to conceal her duplicity from her own conscience.

Clutching her basket to her, she tore her eyes away and fled with hurried steps to the Yellow Salon.

~~~&~~~

"Lizzy, say you will not!" Jane demanded in a scandalized voice.

"I most certainly will," her sister replied with a haughty look that quickly dissolved into laughter that Jane, with a blush at her own credulity, soon joined.

Plying her needle amidst the lively, yet homely companionship of Lizzy and her sister, Georgiana paused a moment to observe their playful manner with each other. The subject had been her Aunt Catherine's latest letter, arrived before the storm, and how Lizzy would respond.

The letter had not been addressed to Elizabeth. Aunt Catherine wrote only to Fitzwilliam what she wished any of them to know. Upon its arrival, they had listened to its contents read-out by her brother in the droll manner he always adopted with their aunt's pronouncements, negating the sting they invariably contained. Fitzwilliam had finished it with a recommendation that its contents be ignored for the most part. Apparently, Georgiana observed, Elizabeth had kept her own counsel and saved it up to be relished with Jane.

She smiled at their play at a reply that would never be made. Fitzwilliam handled all correspondence with their aunt, even for herself, except for the occasional note of gratitude. Lizzy's depiction of a response, delivered in the same tone as the original, was enormously witty. She could almost laugh at it had not each chime of the quarter recalled a haunting vision of Bastien, alone and waiting for her in the library.

A knock and the opening of the Salon door revealed Nurse and a footman carrying a large, blanket-draped basket.

"Four o'clock, ma'am." She curtsied and directed the footman to put his burden at the mistress's side. "Master Alexander is awake." They were all close enough to peek inside the basket at the newcomer. Indeed, he was awake, but blithely unconcerned with his mama or his aunts.

"He looks to be wholly taken up with his fist," Lizzy observed and drew back. "Perhaps I should get on with my needlework while I still may, for I am quite at his command, you know."

Jane settled back into her chair as well and, returning to her knitting, pulled out a length from the ball of wool at her side. Perversely, the ball jumped from there to roll across the room.

"Oh!" she cried after it, just as the door opened again, this time admitting the Comte. Poised with her needle in the air, Georgiana started, fixed by his presence in a room she had considered safely excluded from it.

He stepped into the room with a small bow. "*Votre pardon*," he rose, apologizing for his intrusion, but the wayward ball caught his attention. With a laugh, he strode after it and scooped it up. "*Une boule coquine!*" He held it up. "Madame Bingley, your naughty ball, yes?" He began rewinding it back to her."

"Naughty ball?" Lizzy questioned him.

"Is it not the correct word?" the Count responded and presented the subdued yarn to Jane. "Madame."

"Ah, it is what *ma mère* would call it," he explained. "'*Bastien, apportez-moi la boule coquine, s'il vous plaît*' she would say. As a boy I helped her often with the *tricot*, the knitting? Making the balls…" He made the motion with his hands then, with two fingers, made a running motion across his arm. "And chasing after them."

His simple manner and comic portrayal worked to lessen Georgiana's unease, diminishing it so that she was able to laugh quietly alongside her companions.

"You must have been a great comfort to her," Jane offered, her sincerity bringing a soft flush to the Comte's features.

"*Oui*, Madame Bingley, I think it was so…I hope—" He stopped, seemingly overcome by memories, then looked about for a chair. "May I?"

"Please do," Elizabeth returned, then warned, "but I fear you may find our women's company a bit tedious…unless you wish to take up needlework of your own."

He smiled at her, shaking his head. "*Non, Madame*, I am too out of practice."

"Well," she suggested, returning him a roguish grin, "perhaps Jane could drop some more naughty balls." As they laughed again, a cry arose from the basket.

"Ah, *le bébé!*" Bastien started up from his chair. "He wishes to...to," he stopped in some embarrassment. "Shall I alarm the servant?" His concern was greeted with another gale of laughter.

"No, no, do not 'alarm' Nurse," Elizabeth managed to choke out. "Do not even ring the bell for her. Alexander only wants for attention," she assured him. "His fist no longer entertains." She bent over and tried to rock the basket, but the young master would have none of the mere jiggle she achieved.

"*Permettez-moi,* Madame Darcy." With an outstretched hand, Bastien detained her from rising. "*Le divertissement est mon côté forte.*" He crouched down at the basket and extended a finger to the fussing infant.

Georgiana looked at him in wonder. *A baby?*

"*Bonjour, petit,*" he addressed Alexander in a low voice. "See, he holds my finger! We are friends!" he laughed softly. But as infants are wont to do, Alexander lost his grip, and began to wave his arms frantically and resume crying. "*Non, non, mon petit*! Your friend is still here." Bastien stood and lifted the basket to a table.

Elizabeth sat up straighter and put aside her embroidery, but the Comte's strong hands were already down in the basket. "Bastien, there is no need—"

Her eyes wide in amazement, Georgiana rose from her own chair without thinking and advanced a step toward them. *He is going to pick him up!*

"*Le petit Alexandre* begs to differ, *Madame*. There is every need." Trailing blankets, Bastien lifted the infant from the basket and cradled him in his arms. His finger was grasped once more, the crying ceased, and Bastien looked up in a modest show of triumph, his gentle smile, at the last, alighting upon Georgiana.

She knew herself to be undone.

~~~&~~~

December 17, 1813
Dear Lord Brougham,

Georgiana wrote the entry into her diary, but her thoughts...her emotions from the day even now cascaded through her with such raw insistence that she could only stare at what she had written.

What could I write to him, even in pretence? She concentrated, in her mind forcing a string of words into a line. It was useless; no matter how she arranged them, they did no justice to her heart. Returning her quill to the inkpot, she sat back in her chair and eyed the diary. Her heart clenched and with it came a sudden contempt.

It is all foolishness; these letters...child's play!

She rose from the diary and, scorning its past comfort, closed it sharply and consigned it to a low shelf. *How could you think of "confessing" to Brougham? What could he know of love?*

Chapter 12

Saturday, December 18, 1813

R eluctantly leaving the warmth of his wife's side, Darcy rose from their bed and surveyed the newly-born day from his window. Replete with a rising sun that promised to light a high, blue sky, the scene before him spoke of a crispness that would encourage the day's tasks be set upon with a will.

And, Lord be praised, he peered up at the few hard-edged clouds, *no snow!*

He sighed and broke from the window. Last evening had been the most uncomfortable he had ever spent in his own drawing room. It had not begun well. Upon entering his dressing room to be prepared for dinner, Fletcher had met him with a dejected air.

"Nothing?" he'd asked, without preamble.

"Nothing of great moment," his valet replied. Annoyance with his lack of success was marked in his voice and clipped movements as he set out Darcy's evening clothes. "I *can* tell you that he is English and has spent time on the continent in the past, yet his idea of fashion is deficient if not antiquated." He sniffed in disdain. "I do not believe he has been with the Comte for very long...a year, perhaps more."

"And that is all?"

"Curiously, he appears deathly afraid of the driver, or what the driver may report to His Grace, the Count's father." Fletcher went to work creating a knot with Darcy's cravat. "A reversal of deference the like of which I have *never* encountered."

"Hmm," Darcy responded as the knot was tied. He lowered his chin. Fletcher shook out the evening's frockcoat and held it up. "Anything else?"

"I *will* say this, what the man lacks in art he compensates for in loyalty. He indulges in no gossip of his own nor in that of Pemberley's staff." He paused, then with a grudging tone added, "Any regard I have for him is in the pride he takes in dressing his master. But with such a beautiful young man, how could he not?"

With that accolade ringing in his ears, he stepped into the hall to await his wife. She was before him, however, and appeared to have been pacing the area outside their chamber door.

"Elizabeth!" He advanced to her and reached for her hand.

"My dear, I had no recourse," her confession tumbled out in a rush. "I sent for Georgiana to join Jane and me in the Yellow Salon as you asked."

"She would not come?" he interrupted her in alarm.

"No, she came and all was well." She shook her head. "But later Bastien appeared at the door and what could I do? He was not to know that it was the lady's salon!"

"So, he was with all of you this afternoon." He shut his eyes for a moment then, looking down into her distressed countenance he added, "I should have made sure of him. He was his charming self, I suppose?"

"More, I fear. Nurse had brought Alexander and he started to cry..."

Darcy froze, anticipating her next words.

"...and Bastien picked him up and cajoled him into good humour ... as if he'd been doing so all his life. It was truly beyond anything!"

"Georgiana?" he asked sharply.

Elizabeth nodded. "The look upon her face...well, there he was, as beautiful as—

"Yes," he cut her off brusquely. "What could you have done?" He placed her hand on his arm. "Shall we go down?"

The evening meal had been unusually quiet until Bingley came to the rescue with an entertaining account of time spent with Bastien in contest upon the ice that afternoon. By inference, Darcy placed it before the salon visit, which had not yet been mentioned.

"Then, when Georgiana joined us, we practiced dancing. Jane," Bingley addressed his wife, "when you are able, you must learn! If only there were music, we could have a ball. Imagine! A Christmas Ball on ice!"

Darcy stiffened and shot a look of question at Elizabeth, who indicated her surprise at this as well. As he was able, he observed his sister. She had been quiet, often looking down during the meal and contributing little to the conversation. Alas, he saw that now, when she raised her head, her expression suggested a highly agreeable secret.

Forgoing a separation of the party, they adjourned to the drawing room where brandy was poured for the gentlemen and sherry or tea was served to the ladies. It was not long before there was a certain hum about the room. Nothing voiced, not exactly tension, it was more akin to the expectancy at a hunt where one could only wait for the quarry to break, not knowing in which direction it might spring. It made him exceedingly uncomfortable.

Taking a sip of his brandy, Darcy addressed it directly. "Bastien, I understand that you braved the Yellow Salon this afternoon. Quite extraordinary!"

The Count laughed, "*Pas si courageux*...not so brave. I did not know it was a salon for the ladies only. I inquired of a servant where Madame Darcy could be found and was shown the room." With a lift of his shoulders, he passed off the incident.

"I must congratulate you on the birth of your heir," he continued, tipping his glass toward Darcy. "Such a little fellow he is! We are *amis tout suite,* friends at once, as you say."

"As you say," he had murmured with a tip of his own brandy, his jaw clenching as his back went up at the man's familiarity. A touch of a hand upon his arm had drawn his attention away to his wife, saving him from uttering the incivility that hovered upon his lips. "Thank you," he returned instead with a nod and then ground out, "Uncommonly gracious of you to pay him such notice."

"*Mon plaisir*," Bastien bowed. "My pleasure. An heir...*très important*, non"

Obliged to meet courtesy with courtesy, he returned the bow. With additional words of indebtedness, Elizabeth took the Comte off to see an old Dutch painting that hung across the room. As he watched, Georgiana drifted over to where they stood.

"Charles," he called out, "Shall we excuse ourselves from the ladies in favour of cards? Bastien?"

The next morning nothing had improved save the weather, if it held. Despite rising early after a restless night, Fletcher awaited him in his dressing room.

"Nothing more, I suppose?" Darcy asked, pulling his waistcoat down into place after a quarter hour broken only by the requirements of his attire.

"Alas, no sir. It was late when you came up from cards and I have not seen the Comte's man as yet this morning. But the day is still before us. 'Once more unto the breach' may 'tell thou the tale.'"

"Henry the Fifth? Hmph!" he snorted. "I should wish for even a modicum of his assurance!"

Fletcher nodded at his identification, "And The Taming of the Shrew, sir" His countenance revealed a hint of satisfaction as he rang the kitchen bell and then opened the hall door for him.

Darcy paused. "Two in one, Fletcher!"

"It seemed appropriate, sir."

Darcy strode through the hall and hurried down the stairs in hopes of a solitary breakfast. The tea and toast were just being set upon the table when he arrived to a blessedly empty room.

"The rest will be served shortly, sir," the footman assured him.

"Excellent," he replied and signalling him to pour the tea, he reached for a piece of buttered toast from the rack. With it came a scrap of paper stuck to the back that then fluttered to the table. *What?* He frowned at it but did not move to take it up until the door closed behind the footman's back, whereupon he snatched up the scrap and opened it.

> *In the stables.*
> *D*

~~~&~~~

With a gulp of his tea, Darcy sprang up and followed the footman through the servant's door. The landing behind it gave way to stairs descending to the kitchens to the left and he could still hear the footman clattering down them. The stairs up to the family's hall lay to the right. It was these he ascended at a run and, gaining the hall, slipped through the door to his dressing room.

Empty! He grabbed a coat and hat fit for the stables and returned to the servant's stairs, descending to the kitchen level but turning down a passage to the service door which gave way to the outside. Once out in the air that was every bit as cold as he had guessed, he walked at no more than a swift pace to the stables should anyone observe him and wonder.

The stable appeared deserted. Moving quickly down the centre aisle of horses, he found Dy in the rearmost stall, brushing down one who he'd already supplied with feed.

"Dy!" he bellowed, immense gratitude seeping through him. "Good Lord, I'm glad to see you! How did you get here so soon?"

Dy looked up from the brush he was sweeping over the horse's flank and smiled. "No 'how are you,' Darcy? I am near frozen to death, thank you."

"Come into the house, then! Why the note to meet out here?"

Dy lay the brush aside and caressed the horse's neck. "Good boy," he crooned. "This animal is a hero, Darcy. Getting here was brutal, but he never faltered. I believe I may buy him from the establishment he languished in. He deserves better, let me tell you."

"Undoubtedly," Darcy replied and kept silent. Dy would answer when he was ready. Interrogating him would only prolong the wait for answers.

"You didn't happen to bring something hot with you, I suppose?" At Darcy's conscience-stricken look, he shrugged his shoulders and opened the stall gate. "Too much to be expected, I suppose, but I hope remedied soon? The bit about being near frozen to death is not an exaggeration." He stamped his booted feet on the hard ground of the aisle and peered closely at his friend.

"Come, you *are* that worried, aren't you?" He threw his arms around Darcy in a brief embrace and then clapped him hard on an arm. "I see that the sooner I answer your questions, the sooner something hot may appear, so here it is. How did I get here so soon? I was given leave by the Home Office and decided there was no better place to spend Christmas than Pemberley. You know how I enjoy surprising you, so I did not send ahead. I was already on my way when young Dan Garston and I crossed paths at the Blue Goose near Birmingham where, by the way, the snow began to appear, slowing me considerably."

Darcy shook his head. "I hoped it had not snowed much past Derbyshire, but to meet Garston's son—"

"Providential, I know. It helped that I recognized him! Looks like his father." He paused and, glancing about, saw a horse blanket which he snatched up and flung over his shoulders. "Now, 'why out here?'" He shook his head at him in dismay. "Darcy, old man, what have I always told you?"

"Know your ground," Darcy rolled his eyes. "Idiot!" he castigated himself.

"That may still be, although I'd had hopes!" Dy teased, but then his face grew serious. "But, tell me quickly before I lose consciousness, my friend. What *is* the ground?"

It was entirely too cold to continue in the stables so, shedding the horse blanket, Dy followed Darcy's lead back into Pemberley House through the servant's door and into the warren of rooms below stairs.

"I'll leave you in Reynolds's office while I get something for you," Darcy advised him in a low voice. "No one will come upon you here except Reynolds himself. I'll warn him if I can, but you know him well enough that you can tell him whatever you like and he'll take it as gospel." He pulled the office door toward him and ushered Dy into the small but tidy room. "Oh, Lord! I am glad you are here!" he sighed in earnest and left him to scavenge the kitchen.

The kitchen proved to be a hive of activity in preparation for the morning meal. Darcy slipped into the servant's dining hall and found a number of steaming bowls of porridge and pots of coffee at hand for the moment after those above stairs had been served. Grabbing what he could, he hurried back to Reynold's office and sat down across the butler's desk while his friend dug into the provender.

"Tell me," Dy said simply after several gulps of coffee and a mouthful of porridge.

"First, you tell me what you know of the Comte and his father, the Duc de Fronsac!"

Dy shook his head and looked at him sternly. "Tell me," he repeated, bringing another spoonful of porridge to his mouth. "From the beginning and only facts. Your speculations are not of interest to me at the moment."

Startled by his tone, Darcy frowned but complied. "The Comte's driver appeared at my door very late on Wednesday evening claiming that there had been a carriage accident near our gate . . ." he began and told him what he knew up to the previous evening. It was not until the end of his narrative that, with hesitancy, he broached what he knew would be the painful subject of

Georgiana's increasing fascination with the young Comte.

"Makes love to her at every turn, does he?" Dy responded lightly. A year previously he had confessed his deep and abiding love for his friend's sister despite the years that stood between them and Darcy had sworn him to silence on it. A season, Darcy had demanded of him, perhaps two before he would give him leave to pay his address. Until then he was only to serve her as a friend, a mentor in the hazardous circles of the *ton*.

Darcy watched him closely but, save for the barest of pauses, his friend continued to down the hot food and drink and pepper him with questions.

"Very good," Dy sighed as he pushed away his bowl. He drained the last of the coffee. "Might there be a place I could rest for a few hours? I rode straight here and through the night, you know. Preferably down here," he added, "where I may have some privacy and access to the outside."

"Why—?"

"I need a few hours of sleep and time to think about what you have related," he paused for a heartbeat, "and then, about who I shall be." He grinned wickedly at his old friend. "Even if it is as myself!"

Chapter 13

Admitting Reynolds into their confidence, for the old butler was not to be taken in by two he knew so intimately, Darcy placed his friend into his care for a quiet place to rest and reflect and made his way back to the breakfast room. Bingley, Bastien, and Georgiana were all engaged at table and deep in plans for the day's amusement. A proposal for a sleigh ride over Pemberley's fields was at the top of the list for, it was one of the few outdoor activities that Elizabeth and Jane could join.

"The vistas of a snow-bound Derbyshire in pursuit of fresh air would be just the thing for all of us!" Bingley crowed, delighted at the enthusiasm for his idea.

Filling his plate at the sideboard, Darcy quickly agreed. It would remove everyone from the house for several hours and allow Dy to establish his plans and determine his entrance into Pemberley. "Early afternoon, then?"

"Oh, yes!" Georgiana affirmed, with a glance at Bastien that worked to moderate Darcy's satisfaction with the idea. It was the perfect way forward for Dy. He persuaded himself to disregard the light in her eyes and the anticipation in Bastien's answering smile.

"What will you do in the meantime?" Darcy inquired of those at the table, feeling a sudden urgency to know where everyone would be disposed before Dy made his entry in whatever form that might be.

"Letters!" Bingley replied with a growl, "to my steward and to my sisters. This snow has set me behind in my correspondence, for which my sisters will not forgive me. A minute description of Christmas-tide at Pemberley was ordered and so it must be. Then, Jane has planned a slow stroll around your Gallery for us. Heard there are some 'wonderful paintings' to be appreciated." He made a face, then added quickly, "All are welcome to join us."

"*Oui*, Charles. I will be most pleased to see the wonderful *peintures*. *Une* galerie d'art, how enchanting!" the Comte exclaimed, leaning forward. "*Mademoiselle* Darcy, will you also take the slow stroll among the arts?"

"I think ... I hope I may," she stuttered. "Mrs. Darcy and I have an appointment with Cook this morning to review menus and stores for next ... for Christmas. Because of the snow ..." Her voice trailed off in the face of Bastien's evident disappointment. What did he care for the details of housewifery? He wanted her company. He wanted ... her. "I will try."

His smile was beatific. "*Bon!*"

"And you, Bastien?" Darcy pinned him with a curious glance.

"Ah, I think I will speak with Grayson, my driver," he clarified to the others, "and discover his opinion of repairs. Is it possible letters be sent north?" No one at the table could give him an answer. "Perhaps, I send Grayson to Lambton for news."

This was the first time the Comte had expressed any interest in his own affairs and Darcy would have welcomed it had Bastien's plans not threatened to bring him into the environs of servants and stable. "Allow me to send into Lambton for you," he offered.

"*Non, non*, I will speak with Grayson. And then we shall see the *peintures, oui*?" His gaze encompassed them all.

Darcy rose from the table and the rest followed suite, each happily anticipating the projected sleighing expedition across Pemberley's snowy acres. Hanging back, Darcy watched them make their ways up the stairs, pursing his lips as the Comte attentively drew Georgiana up on his arm. When they all had disappeared, he took himself down to the kitchens to inform Dy of the plans.

Brougham was not in Reynolds's office, nor for that matter was Reynolds. Startling a servant unused to encountering his master below stairs, he determined from him that Reynolds was in the wine cellar.

"To the wine cellar," he muttered to himself, a bit alarmed that his allies had become so elusive. But then, again, Dy … And the wine cellar was, actually, a good location. Only Reynolds possessed the key and that, on his person. No one would surprise them there.

A soft rap of his knuckles on the wine cellar door was answered by the appearance of Reynolds's eye and followed by a finger to the butler's lips. He opened the door enough for Darcy to slip inside where he could see a tidy servant's mattress spread on the floor with Dy lying upon it, covered with quilts and, seemingly, dead to the world.

Darcy looked down upon his sleeping friend, wondering if he had ever before seen him in repose. It was not likely. Dy was always so vibrant, so up to everything, that the lines across his brow and around his mouth seemed to belong to some other creature. He looked tired, very, very tired. And why not? He'd ridden all night in beastly weather to come to his aid ... or, rather, to Georgiana's aid, truth be told. And his hair! He had not noticed before, maybe because of a cap, but the bushy hair on the top of his friend's head and that hung shaggily over his brow had turned grey: stark, raving grey! When had *that* happened? *Why* had it happened?

Darcy shook his head and glancing at Reynolds, indicated that they leave the room. Let him get some sleep ... some peace.

Reynolds closed the door behind them, but did not lock it, trusting in the regard of the staff concerning the relationship of the head butler with the wine to keep them from the door. "He was exhausted, sir. Almost dropped at my feet."

"You did well, Reynolds. Just the place for him. Anything he wants, you understand?" They reached the butler's office and once inside, Darcy reached for a pen and paper, quickly scribbling a note. "Give him this and keep me informed if you can, but do not be concerned should he disappear. Lord Brougham knows what he is about."

"Yes, sir." A wary grimace flashed across Reynolds's face. "And well I know."

On his way up to the family's floor, Darcy considered who he should tell about Dy's presence at Pemberley. Dy had said that no one should know for the present. Would Bingley and Jane recognize him? Certainly not *en costume* should he appear in disguise. They knew Dy only slightly as his friend from university days and nothing about his past with His Majesty's Home Office. Georgiana might see beyond the paint and pose should he try it. Elizabeth? He took a deep breath as he closed upon their bedchamber door. *What should you do about Elizabeth?*

Inside the door, Elizabeth's Annie was completing the final touches on her mistress's coiffure. His wife's eyes met his in the mirror before her as she cast him a wry smile that called forth one of his own. *How did she manage to be so beautiful?* A burble of sound pulled his attention to the cradle set before the sun lit window.

"Yes, he is still awake, the little scoundrel!" she laughed, choosing her favourite opal ear drops and matching necklace. The tiny diamonds set either side of the stone flashed as Annie slipped it around her neck. She rose from the dressing table and together they went to the cradle. "Did you wish to see your Papa before your nap?" Arms and legs moved with vigour if not purpose under the blanket.

"Of course, he does!" Darcy bent and scooped up his son, still milky-sweet from his morning feeding. "We have matters to discuss, do we not, Alexander?'

"Not serious ones, I hope," Elizabeth teased, but her words gave him pause. He looked down into those fine eyes, the genesis of his fall into the love and companionship he'd despaired of ever finding. If he were to say anything about Dy, now would be the time.

"Fitzwilliam?"

He settled Alexander into the crook of his arm. "No," he crooned down into the tiny face, "nothing serious at all."

~~~&~~~

Several hours later, an ancient underling from the house appeared at the stable workroom door bearing in his palsy-rattled hands a tray piled with baskets of fresh bread and butter. Attending them was a deep pitcher of something that sent fragrant drifts of steam through the air. Shuffling to the centre of the room, the old man set it down with deliberate care on the long table that served as workbench, dinner table, and dice board.

"What's this?" One of the grooms rose with a girth strap he was repairing and surveyed the offerings set before them. "Oi," he called to the others scattered about the room. "Smell that? Fresh bread and, glory be, if it ain't spiced hard cider in that pitcher." Interest turned into a general rush to the table, but one that carefully avoided the Comte's man, who appeared unmoved by the remarkable display of largesse.

Questions of why the food had appeared were adequately met with a shrug and something about the extra work in preparing the sleighs for the afternoon as all but the Frenchman's driver dug in. Gradually, the others drifted off to duties or preparations for the sleighing expedition. The stable yard soon rang with the hooves of those horses chosen to pull the sleighs and the noise of their groomers as they brushed and braided them to advantage.

The doorway darkened for a moment, and the old man looked up from a saddle he'd begun to oil and blinked rheumy eyes. A young man, obviously a guest at the House, entered the workroom and pausing briefly to survey its shadowy interior, made for the driver of the French Comte's coach. The ancient grunted his unconcern with the vagaries of his betters and returned to his task.

"Grayson!" the gentleman spoke urgently to the driver who had retained his seat, exhibiting not the least intention of rising in his master's presence, let alone bowing. The young man pushed a stool over to the driver and sat down, his shoulder's hunched. "Have you heard from His Grace?" he asked in unaccented English.

"*Parlez en français. Nous pouvons être entendus,*" Grayson hissed at him.

The younger man's eyes widened. "There's no reason to be surly!" He gazed about, noting the grizzled old man working on saddlery across the room but immediately discounting him. "There's no one here."

"No, I have heard nothing more from your father, so you are to continue until you have secured her."

"But more guests, relatives of the family, are to arrive on Tuesday when we are to drive into the village to meet—

"And so ...?"

"Darcy is trouble enough! More curious relatives to disarm, some of which were with her for her Season? More questions? The men from the village may remember me and wonder—

"Continue to be your charming self, Bastien." Grayson responded with undisguised sarcasm. "It is your singular talent and one upon which His Grace has placed all his hopes."

An angry storm appeared and played across Bastien's countenance. "He should not have placed this entirely upon me! 'All his hopes?'"

Grayson did not respond.

He tried another tack. "Darcy is suspicious that I have not done more about the coach and that no letters have arrived for me from York."

"What has a Comte to do with coach repairs? You worry too much, Bastien."

"And you worry not at all!" He reversed course once again, "Look here, I have received no letters from His Grace or from those handling the sale of the estate. It does not sit right with Darcy, I tell you."

"The snow," was Grayson's only response.

"*Ah, Sacré bleu!*" Bastien threw up his hand in frustration.

"*Nous parlons donc maintenant en français?*" Grayson straightened in his chair. "Or will you only use it to swear against God?" He returned to his care-naught slouch. "I will supply letters."

The stormy look transfigured into mutiny. His voice was tight. "What am I to do?"

"*Secure her*! Make love to her and anyone else you must. *C'est une jolie innocente*. If you cannot seduce such a child into a consensual engagement—

"Seduce!" Bastien interrupted him in disgust.

"You *know* what His Grace said. Her dowry and inheritance will be the same and fall to us equally through consent or necessity."

"*C'est horrible!*" Bastien rose from the table.

"*La Révolution aussi, Neveu,*" replied his uncle.

Chapter 14

Like Chatsworth House, the seat of the Duke of Devonshire, Pemberley House, and particularly it's art gallery, was featured as a sight not to be missed in Miss Wordsworth's *Recollections of a Tour Made in the Derbyshire Dales*. "A result of more than a hundred years of meticulous attention," the guide read, "the Darcy family could be justly proud of the collection." Darcy and Elizabeth were not strangers to its delights, and strolling slowly among its canvases had been a particular pleasure during the months of her confinement.

Darcy paced the wide hall before the gallery doors, a note from Reynolds in his hand. "A certain person is not to be found" it read, and despite his assurances to his butler, he was worried. At best, Dy had gotten but two hours of sleep! Now he was gone without a word.

Footsteps echoed down the hall, warning him that his guests were approaching. Stuffing the note into a pocket, he wrapped his arms across his chest in a bid to restrain his disquiet. In moments, Georgiana emerged from around the corner, an eager light animating her face. Her brisk steps faltered when she saw that he alone awaited her and the anticipation in her eyes faded. Slower now, she joined him at the door.

"Bastien has not arrived? You have not seen him?" she asked.

"No, I have been here alone some minutes." He tried to keep his voice even, but the implication of her questions ... "Georgiana, you did not consent to an assignation—

"No!" She looked at him, stricken. "Of course not." She looked away and then retraced some of her steps.

Oh, Georgie, Georgie, his brother's heart followed after her. It was not so very long ago that she had confided in him. Now, it seemed as if she was hiding from him, running away. *A little more time!*

A few more minutes brought Bingley, Jane, and his own Elizabeth pushing the most cunning little baby carriage, a present from his aunt, Lady Matlock. Made of rushes and interwoven with ribbons, the basket on wheels skimmed merrily along and would perform admirably for a tour of the gallery. Its cheerfulness made him smile, and the satisfaction in Elizabeth's face tempted him to laugh.

"Is it not the perfect thing?" Bingley addressed his friend. "I have never seen the like! We must get one before our baby arrives!"

"My dear Charles," Jane smiled gently at his enthusiasm. "Never seen one? But I suppose you have not frequented the London parks during the nursery hour."

"I should say not!" he replied. "But you must admit that this one is beyond charming."

A whimpering sound emerged from the depths of the carriage. "Shall we begin?" Darcy indicated the doors. "Alexander, you see, is very fond of movement. We have been stationary too long."

"But Bastien is not yet arrived." Georgiana looked up at her brother.

"I am sure he will find his way soon, Sweetling. You are needed. Come with us," he took her arm and gently drew her along with the others. "You know the gallery so well," he added as they followed Elizabeth and the carriage, the doors closing behind them.

~~~&~~~

The fact that both the Comte and Dy were missing at the same time took possession of Darcy's mind as they strolled among the paintings and statuary. It could be just a coincidence, of course, but he itched to affirm or disprove it, and truth be told, he looked over his shoulder quite as often as his sister for the approach of the absent Comte.

The apprehension of both of them was finally relieved a half hour into their stroll when a breathless Comte trotted up to them. Georgiana visibly relaxed and her countenance returned to its brightness of before as Bastien addressed her with a bow.

"*Pardon, mademoiselle. Je suis un idiot*," he begged her. "I was speaking with my driver and he wished me to examine one of our horses. 'Immediately!' he says. There was much, ah... and it was required to change the clothes and boots."

"We are almost finished here," Darcy responded, looking over Bastien's dress. "A luncheon repast will be served as soon as we are done. The sleighs will be ready at two o'clock."

"*Excellent,*" Bastien exclaimed and held out his arm to Georgiana.

"What was wrong with the horse?" Darcy forestalled him.

For a moment, Bastien's face expressed incomprehension and in the next, a flicker of alarm rippled over his visage. Darcy cocked his head, his brow now raised at the Comte's difficulty with an answer.

"*C'était ... c'était une ecchymose.* A ... a bruise. *Pardon,* I could not remember the English." Bastien offered and his smile returned. "A bruise has appeared on the leader's hock."

"Ah," Darcy responded. "What was your conclusion?"

"*Ce n'est rien de grave* ...nothing so grave. In a few days, it will mend, *merci.*" He turned again to Georgiana and once more offered his arm. "*Mademoiselle* Darcy, will you show me, until luncheon, the beautiful paintings?"

~~~&~~~

As Georgiana followed Elizabeth and Jane up the stairs to change, she knew herself to be almost giddy with excitement. Luncheon had been a merry time of anticipation of the afternoon's excursion. The beauty if what they would see was the expectation on the women's side and exaggerations of probable speed on the speculation of the men. Then, when the meal ended, Bastien had accompanied her to the foot of the stairs with whispered designs of claiming a seat beside her in one of the sleighs. She had happily agreed and now was determined to make it so.

Barrow had everything laid out for her approval and she joyfully affirmed all her choices. Her green wool pelisse was replaced with a scarlet one of velvet with a matching bonnet, both trimmed in white rabbit fur, that had been a present from Elizabeth last year. Warmer stockings and petticoats were added under her dress and shiny black leather boots with woollen socks lay beside her dressing chair. The muff from skating lay on her bed to be taken up as soon as a striking scarlet, blue, and cream paisley shawl was draped across her arms.

"There now, Miss," Barrow whispered and turned her toward the mirror. "You look the veriest angel of Christmas!"

Blushing at such a description, Georgiana raised her eyes to the mirror in critical appraisal but, to her astonishment, found she could not disagree! Oh, not that she was any sort of angel, but that the image in the mirror was exceptional, the best self she had ever beheld!

Is it love? She asked her mirrored self. She cast her mind back two years when she had thought herself in love once before. *No, it is not the same.* Then, she had been wracked with feelings of inadequacy, easily lead, and hushed into secrecy.

Secrecy? The word put a sudden point to her self-examination. *Secrecy?*

A knock at her door brought her back to the present. Barrow excused herself and went to answer it. "Yes, sir. Yes, she is ready." She opened the door wide to admit her mistress's brother, himself dressed with an eye to warmth and his valet's idea of quiet elegance.

"Georgiana!" he exclaimed at the sight of her. "Come, my girl. You shall dazzle us all and bewitch the horses!"

"Fitzwilliam!" she responded with a giggle. "How can you say such a thing when it is you who look 'every inch a king.'"

"Are you ready?"

"Yes," she reached out and took his hand. Darcy turned her out into the hall where Elizabeth awaited them.

"The two loveliest women of my acquaintance!" He kissed them on their foreheads. "The horses are waiting."

~~~&~~~

The Comte was not awaiting her at the foot of the stairs as Georgiana had expected. Feigning unconcern, she remained on her brother's arm, trusting in Bastien's ingenuity to arrange the seating. The footmen opened the doors to the courtyard and the confirmation of the brilliant promise of perfect sleighing weather that had excited them from the windows of Pemberley House.

Stationed at the far side of the second sleigh, Bastien looked up to her with a wide smile and then with eyes that fully conveyed his utter worship of what he beheld. So intense was his regard that her pleasure with it warmed her from head to foot. Casting her eyes down to the steps to watch her step, she descended the portico stairs. With her attention firmly on her feet, she nearly walked into one of the stable hands occupied with adjusting the harnessing and lay of the reins.

"'Scuse me, Miss," a rough voice startled her into attending to the scene around her. Instinctively, she took a step back but in doing so, one of her heels rocked on an uneven cobblestone. Arms flailing, she struggled to regain her balance as a chorus of alarm arose from those in the courtyard.

A pair of strong, gloved hands gripped her shoulders and settled her back squarely on her feet. "Easy now, Miss!" the voice above her cautioned and the hands released her.

"Th-thank you," she responded and looked up to see who it was that had rescued her from possible harm and certain embarrassment. But his back was to her already, and only a sprig of holly in his knitted cap distinguished him from the others who worked the stables.

"*Mademoiselle*! You must take care!" Bastien's alarm diverted her attention away from the retreating figure. "*Venez, s'il vous plaît*, allow me to escort you."

"How could I be so clumsy?" she said to herself, not meaning anyone to hear. They did not escape the Comte's attention.

"That, you could *never* be," he denied in a whisper, but his hold on her was firm as he assisted her into the sleigh. Vaulting in beside her, he met a surprised Darcy standing on the other side.

"You wish to go with the ladies?" Darcy was incredulous, then considered that he should have anticipated such a move. How was he to pry the man out of the sleigh and away from Georgiana's side? "It will be very slow-going, Bastien. Stop-and-look the whole way out, I imagine." The Comte only smiled at him. Darcy tried another approach. "I've had our fastest pair harnessed to the other sleigh and they are in rare form."

"*Merci*, Darcy, *mais je suis content*."

Darcy was compelled to admit defeat as he helped Elizabeth and then Jane ascend the steps to the sleigh's plush cushions and settle in opposite his sister and the Comte. There was not enough room to join them and neither his wife nor sister-in-law should hazard the other sleigh to make room in this one. *And it would be a dead bore!* he thought, comparing in his mind their slow pace to the anticipated power of the two animals harnessed to the other sleigh.

How much could happen? He reached out to pat Elizabeth's hand in farewell, but at the last moment squeezed it instead and met her look with one of his own that she well understood. With a slight nod, her eyes slid to the couple opposite her and then back to her husband.

The taut state of Darcy's emotions eased with her silent assurance. He could not say that their harmony was complete. What couple could boast of that after only a year of marriage? But the extent of it, especially in regard to Georgiana, still surprised him. She was his helpmeet in everything, whether they were in unexceptional concord or not.

He strode to the second sleigh and mounted the steps into it but refrained from sitting until he had surveyed the courtyard. Except for the stable worker who had caught Georgiana before she fell, the only other occupants of the courtyard were busy shovelling up the evidence of waiting horses. He sat down with a frown that was jerked from him with the snap of a whip as the horses jumped forward into their collars. They were off, but not before the question reoccurred to plague him—

Where was Dy, anyway; and what, in heaven's name was he doing?

<center>~~~&~~~</center>

The sleigh ride was a success, as Darcy counted it. Upon their return, he helped Elizabeth down before the stairs into Pemberley House and was gladdened to see its effects. She had not been out of doors for two weeks before Alexander was born. It had done her good as evidenced by the rose of her cheeks and the care-free laughter in her voice. Anxious as he was to hear her account of the outing, he refrained and trusted that since she exhibited no rush to apprise him, there was little about which to concern himself.

He looked to his sister. There he found another story. She appeared unusually quiet, subdued despite having been out in bracing weather in the company of a young man supposedly in love with her. *What had happened?*

She had no eyes for the Comte. Instead, she looked pensively at her gloved hands while she waited for Bingley to assist his wife from the sleigh. On her rising, Bastien leapt from the sleigh and immediately turned to help her, not with the steps but by placing his hands about her waist. Georgiana stilled and then, surrendering to his importunity, allowed him to lift her down.

Darcy stiffened at this gesture of familiarity and his disquiet increased as he mounted the steps behind them, their hands fluttering between themselves, now touching, now apart. He loudly cleared his throat and the fluttering ceased. It was the outside of enough and he would have a word with Georgiana, that was certain!

The doors opened before them into the hall where footmen and maids divested them of their coats and wraps. Reynolds approached to inform them that refreshments were prepared against their arrival in the Blue Salon and would they care to partake now rather than after they had changed into lighter dress?

"Now!" was the unanimous response and with laughter and appetites sharpened by the cold, they followed Darcy up the stairs to the Salon. The doors were opened for them and wonderful sights and smells of delicious fare met their senses as well as a roaring fire in the hearth.

"Well, it is about time you returned!" a voice arose from a high back chair positioned toward the fire. "I was tempted to begin without you!" Lord Dyfed Brougham rose from the chair with a careless elegance and saluted them with a glass of Darcy's very expensive brandy. "Shall we eat?"

Chapter 15

The room exploded with questions and exclamations of welcome which Lord Brougham accepted with benign patience and wry surprise that his arrival at Pemberley should be the cause of such a to-do.

"Didn't I write to you that I was coming, Darcy? No? Well, my lamentable memory, you know. The very devil of an inconvenience. I was certain that I did!" He smiled in general at all of them. "You do have room, I take it?"

"Of course!" Darcy's grip closed upon Brougham's arm in relief. "Don't be silly!"

"Silly? Now, Darcy, have I *ever*, to your knowledge, been silly?" He paused. "No, I think not. Amusing, perhaps, but not silly, no. At the moment," he continued, looking into the air, "I am not *feeling* amusing, I can tell you. What I am feeling is peckish. Are we going to enjoy your cook's fine efforts or not?"

"Lord Brougham," Elizabeth advanced upon him and drew him to the tables, "how wonderful that you have come! It seems an age since I have seen you! We can hardly thank you enough—"

"Tut, tut, Ma'am," he forestalled her. "Nothing to speak of. A word here, a word there." He shrugged and picked up a plate. "But who is this gentleman that no one has introduced? He *is* a gentleman, I presume." Brougham cast Bastien a maddeningly innocent smile calculated to frustrate the very response his words meant to provoke.

The Comte's visage darkened. He looked to Darcy to make the introduction.

Irrationally heartened at Brougham's unexpected appearance, Georgiana's eyes widened at her friend's deliberate provocation. *What is he about and why has he not yet greeted me?*

"Pardon me," Darcy hurried to amend his oversight. "Le Comte du Pont-Courlay, may I present Lord Dyfed Brougham, Earl of Westmarch. Lord Brougham, the Comte du Pont-Courlay." The two bowed low to each other and, to Bastien's credit, he extended his hand. These societal formalities completed, the two strongly reminded Darcy of a pair of prize fighting cocks squaring off in the ring.

Dy shook it, but tepidly, then handed Bastien a plate. "Hungry?"

"Yes, fainting, Lord Brougham," Bastien accepted the plate as a peace offering but with only a ghost of a smile.

"You must try a piece of this grouse," he offered as if he were the meal's host. "Darcy's cook is a wizard with grouse. Shoot it yourself, Darcy?

"Actually, Georgiana did, before the snow became too deep to hunt."

"Good girl!" Dy looked up and finally smiled at her. His return to the Brougham she knew reassured her and she followed the others in filling their plates.

"So," Brougham began when they'd taken seats. "It appears that the blessed event has taken place. You are now a father, Darcy! My astonished congratulations to you both. Not astonished at you, of course, ma'am," he nodded to Elizabeth, who trilled with laughter at this admission. "You, I have always regarded as quite competent." He left the comment to hang in silence. In a few moments, Bingley began to snicker, then the Comte. Then everyone was laughing, although the humour was somewhat lost upon Georgiana. Darcy merely snorted and shook his head.

"You must not mind him, Bastien," Darcy warned, "You see how he abuses everyone, but especially his friends!"

"Now I see what it is!" Bingley sat back and waved his fork at his lordship. "I've been sitting here thinking *something* was different. Brougham, your hair has gone grey!"

"By Jove, has it?" Dy's hand went up to his crown and ruffled his hair.

"Seriously," Darcy asked when the laughter had subsided, "When did this happen?"

"I do not know! Just brought to my attention...speak to my valet." Brougham looked at him slyly. "Le Comte," he turned to Bastien, "Pont-Courlay... Bordeaux?"

"Before *La Révolution*, yes. Our *château*—

"You must have been very young when it was lost."

"*Oui, Monseigneur,* only three years old."

"Austria?"

Bastien nodded.

"Switzerland or Prussia after that?"

"First Switzerland and then Prussia, as did most *émigrés.* You are very well informed, *Monseigneur!*" Bastien's eagerness to tell his story faded.

"Oh, one picks up things here and there," Brougham waved a hand in dismissal of any particular depth of knowledge. "But how do you come to be here at Pemberley? Derbyshire is not what one would call 'hospitable' to the French, even if they are *émigrés.* They barely tolerate me, and I am merely next door to being Welsh."

"That is only *almost* true," Darcy corrected him with another snort.

"I am on my way to York when the coach, it hits rocks in the road and overturns near Pemberley's gate. A great many repairs are necessary, and the snow…" He lifted his shoulders, indicating his helplessness. "What can one do until the road is open to …" He looked to Darcy.

"Chesterfield," he supplied. "It is the closest town with a carriage builder. We're replacing all we can but have reached the end of what we can supply."

"But I ask you, what is in York, my dear Comte, that you travel there overland this time of year?" Brougham shivered. "I would not have ventured as far north as Derbyshire except my good friend Darcy was expecting me and how could I disappoint him?"

"I was *not* expecting you, remember?"

"Darcy, did I know that?" He turned back to the Comte, his brow lifted in expectation.

"I go to join my father, le Duc du Fronsac, concerning an estate."

"Fronsac!" Brougham whistled under his breath. "That is high, indeed!"

"You know him?" Bastien's eyes were guarded.

"Know *of* him. Your family is not only *from* Bordeaux, it *owned* Bordeaux ...or much of it!"

"No longer, *Monseigneur*." Bastien fell silent.

"*Juste comme ça*," Brougham replied evenly. "Just so." He rose then and returned to the laden table, picking up a bottle of sherry after choosing additional delicacies for his own plate.

"More sherry, Georgiana?" Brougham leaned over her shoulder with the offering. Bastien stilled as Georgiana smiled up at him.

"Only a little. Thank you, my lord."

"Not at all." He pitched his reply at a purr. Its timbre was not lost upon the Comte, nor the familiarity within the exchange. He stirred restively in his chair.

Dy looked over at him from under his brow. Vise-like, the Comte's right hand was gripping the arm of his chair. He unleashed the barest of smiles before looking away. *Challenge delivered ... challenge accepted.*

~~~&~~~

Later, upon Elizabeth's signal, Georgiana and Jane rose with her and excused themselves from the company of the gentlemen. After the men had returned their curtsies and the ladies turned to leave, Georgiana was surprised to hear Bastien beg his host's pardon and hurry toward her into the hall. His disregard for etiquette discomfited her and although her back was to him, Georgiana could sense his urgency to detain her. Elizabeth looked back past her and then directed a quick frown in her direction that communicated more than surprise. She must manage this situation.

"*Mademoiselle* Darcy!" he began and moved to possess himself of her arm. "Georgiana."

"*Monsieur le Comte?*" Georgiana turned to him and addressed him formally with a curtsy and the carefully indifferent expression she had learned this year in London. Would the tenor of her response finally recall him to the proprieties? *And how had he come to grant himself the use of my first name?*

Bastien's countenance transformed from one of surety in his reception to one of disbelief. His face paled and then flushed as the indecorum of his actions were impressed upon him by her response.

"Your pardon, *Mademoiselle*, I feared that you were unwell. You leave so early."

Georgiana bestowed the whisp of a smile upon him. "I am well. There is no cause for concern, *Monsieur*." She held to her part, willing herself to remain calm despite the trembling that raced through her.

He bowed at her response and stepped away.

Alone now in her bed chamber, her conscience flooded in the self-reproach that had arisen to plague her in the sleigh. The small intimacies which she had not discouraged as she had led him through the Gallery had become closer ones as they rode in the sleigh. Hands were held beneath her muff; the sleigh's motion served as an excuse for Bastien to lean into her, perhaps more than was warranted, exclamations were shared that brought his face so close to hers that it was almost a kiss. It had all been exhilarating! But when his hand moved under the lap robe to caress her knee, her mind abruptly cleared with the memory of another time.

Wickham! Her obsession with the Comte collapsed as cold recollection closed about her heart. *What was she thinking? And this man little more than a stranger!* She closed her eyes against the looming enormity of her part in the fault. *You encouraged this!*

But Elizabeth had counselled enjoyment, hadn't she? another part of her hastened to justify. *Was this not merely that?*

A truer voice opposed the wily stratagem. *How could it be if it had led to Bastien so forgetting himself?* She was mortified.

Foolish, foolish girl! What have you done!

~~~&~~~

A soft and not unexpected knock sounded on Darcy's servant's door minutes after Fletcher undertook redressing him for the evening. It opened before Fletcher could reach for the handle. Dy slipped in and closed it gently behind him.

"Well, well." He looked about the room. "I have not been in here since we came that night in search of your father's new shipment of West Indian cheroots! You have not changed it much. Probably not even..." He leaned over a drawer and opened it, releasing a rich tobacco scent to waft into the air. "No, not even where the stock of cheroots is kept." He took several and secured them inside his frock coat.

"Oh, do help yourself! I insist!"

Dy laughed at him and patted his coat, then all humour left his face. "Darcy, we must talk."

"What have you discovered?"

Dy cocked an eye to Fletcher in unspoken question.

"As the grave, my lord," the valet responded solemnly.

"Good man!" Dy nodded. "As I said in the Salon, Le Duc du Fronsac is, or rather was, a highly placed member in Louis's court. I was not being absurd when I said much of Bordeaux was in his *seigneurie*. Their fortune was supported by their control of the region's wine trade, which was lost, of course, in the Revolution."

"Of course," Darcy released a deep breath. "They are merely fortune hunters, then?"

"To be sure, it easily explains the Comte's pursuit of Georgiana which, by the by, is a plot of his father's making; but that is not the sum of it." Dy circled his friend before continuing. His hesitancy caused a pain like the blow of a fist to centre in Darcy's stomach. "You must be aware that not many of Louis's friends remain alive, Darcy. If the Jacobins did not find and execute them under Danton's *Ministère de la Justice*, Fouché and his *Ministère de la Police* will do the same for Napoleon."

Darcy went cold. "Are we in danger?" Fletcher held out his frock coat and Darcy slipped into it, though his attention was firmly set upon his friend.

"Little, I believe," Dy returned, shaking his head "And for that we may thank the Lord for the very snow that deposited the Comte at your gate. Travel to the north is very difficult and south from the closest ports, almost impossible. Even should agents in search of Fronsac arrive in York, they would know nothing of Pemberley. Le Comte has disappeared into the snowy wilds of Derbyshire!" He laughed ironically. "Quite fortunate for him. It may have saved his life!"

"Snow or not, Georgiana is his quarry," Darcy stated rather than asked. "That was certainly underscored in the Blue Salon."

"Yes." Dy replied simply. Then, his reluctance becoming visible, he changed his mind and added, "And if she were somehow to become *attached* to him, she would become party to the *inquiétude* Fronsac and his son represent to the French government."

"Even after all these years?"

"There can be no claimants to the Bordeaux wine trade. Her fortune will finance an establishment here in England until Napoleon is defeated. Then, if Fronsac is still alive or his son is of the same mind, lawsuits in France." He hesitated and bit his lip. "And heirs to press them forward until all resources are consumed."

"What about the Home Office?" Darcy could not contemplate Dy's last words but instead grasped at what little he knew of his friend's commitments. "Do they know of such agents being in England?"

Brougham sighed, "There are *always* French agents in England. I have not heard of any hunting Fransac in particular, but His Majesty's government does not confide *everything* to me, my friend."

A silence fell between them that neither men could bring himself to break.

"You are ready for the evening, sir," Fletcher quietly informed his master, then addressed his friend. "Does my lord have evening clothes at hand?"

Dy directed a wry grin at him. "Fletcher, I regret that I have not. My portmanteaus follow me, but for tonight I have nothing but what I stand in. Something of Darcy's, perhaps, but something with rather more dash, mind you?"

Darcy nodded absently, bestowing the permission requested by the cock of his valet's brow. Fletcher bowed. "It will be my *pleasure* to dress you, my lord!"

"I shall rely upon your excellent taste, Fletcher. Attend me as soon as you can." He opened the servant's door. "Oh, and there are some soiled clothes and boots in my dressing room. Please have them cleaned and returned to their owner."

"Yes, my lord."

"There's a good man. I shall steal you from Darcy yet!"

"Soiled clothes?" Darcy put a hand against the servant's door. "What were you up to all afternoon?"

"Oh, several things." Dy grinned at him. "Keeping my eye on you, for one …," He reached into a pocket and withdrew a sprig of holly which he placed carefully in Darcy's palm. "And catching your sister before she could fall, for another."

Chapter 16

At dinner that evening Lord Brougham extended himself to amuse them from his vast command of news which he embellished with sundry wry observations and the occasional titillating *on dit* fresh from London Society. Despite her subdued frame of mind, Georgiana could not help but laugh along with the others. His sly looks and revelations of the *Ton's* follies and foibles drew her out of herself, freeing her, for the moment, from the self-consciousness of her own.

"Georgiana, my dear," Brougham drawled, "Do you remember young Simon Ledbetter? He hung about you long enough, so I'm sure you must."

"Why, yes, Lord Brougham. Was he not the gentleman with the unruly horse?" Georgiana replied.

"The very one! Darcy," Dy sat forward and looked down the table to his host, "you did not meet him, having come back here for that week; so, Simon Ledbetter was left for *me* to deal with. Nice chap, but not a horseman, except in his own mind, and mad to impress your sister. Did she tell you of this?"

Darcy looked to Georgiana, his curiosity aroused both by the subject and Dy's purpose in introducing the story. "No, she did not!"

"It was nothing, really!" she protested but could not suppress her urge to giggle at the memory.

"May hap to you, my girl, but young Ledbetter was keen, Darcy, *very* keen. Keen enough to lay down four hundred pounds on Goforth's flashy nag for nothing more than to ride it in St. James's Park."

"Good heavens, why? Everyone knows about the Goforth curse. 'The Devil at cards—"

"—but a Babe at horses." Dy finished for him. "Everyone but Ledbetter it would seem. Well, he bought it, and London was agog to see what would happen when he finally appeared in the Park. Two days later, you received a note, did you not, Georgiana?"

While he awaited her reply, Dy flicked another glance at the Comte. Yes, just as he suspected would happen. Every time he said Georgiana's Christian name the man flinched, stirred in his seat, or partook of some wine. *Too young for this sort of work*, he concluded but could feel no pity for him, not when kidnap had been suggested and he had not demurred.

If you will indulge in deep games, Monsieur le Comte, *you must learn how to play them. But are you still dangerous? I think, yes.*

"Yes, I did receive a note," Georgiana confessed, "and I felt so sorry for him that I accepted his invitation to go riding the next day." A feeling of ease enveloped her. *How delightful it is to be part of Lord Brougham's story!*

"Which I scotched immediately that evening!" Brougham added. "You were rather put out with me at the time, I believe."

"I was," Georgiana admitted, "but you were right, the poor man. Lord Brougham directed that I reply to his invitation that I would come to watch him only."

"Brougham is always right." Bingley slapped the table. "Remember last year at the Melbourne's? Saved our skins! Follow his advice any day!"

All eyes were upon Dy, who modestly inclined his head, acknowledging Bingley's accolade, but Georgiana's attention had veered from him to her brother-in-law. *Follow his advice any day.* She looked in wonder at the others. Were they so caught up in Brougham's story that they had not felt the earth shift beneath them? An unconscious wall she had not even known to exist developed a crack and then another.

"What happened at the Melbourne's?" Elizabeth asked. When no one enlightened her, and even Charles kept his own counsel, she asked Brougham directly, "How did you save them?"

"That, dear lady, is for another day. But we were speaking of Georgiana's erstwhile suitor and his new-bought steed. Did I mention the miscreant's name? No? Bullet ... it was Bullet.

"Oh no! You are joking!" Darcy exclaimed.

"I am not."

"What happened next, Monsieur Brougham?" Bastien ventured into the story being woven around them.

"I called for Georgiana and drove her to the Park to *watch* Ledbetter and Bullet. I knew there would be trouble as soon as he appeared on the ground with a groom leading the horse to the track behind him."

"On the ground," Bingley questioned him, "not riding?"

"On the ground," he affirmed. "Ledbetter approached us and asked Georgiana what she thought of the animal. We said all that was proper, for it was a beautiful horse, and with a satisfied air that he had scored points with us, he made his way to it. Do you remember what happened next, my dear?"

Georgiana nodded, "The horse sidestepped his every attempt to mount and almost kicked him." She smiled to herself as the familiar resonance of Brougham's voice swept over her, widening cracks into fissures.

"But Ledbetter was undaunted, determined as he was to impress our Georgiana as husband material. I will give him that." Dy shrugged, glancing at the Comte. "So, *finally* he managed to throw his leg over the beast, who has now begun to dance about, and gather up the reins. He smiles at Georgiana and then nods to his groom, who releases the horse."

Everyone, save Georgiana, held their breaths and waited. She put her hand to her lips to prevent herself from giving anything away, neither the story at hand nor the increasing clarity of her heart.

"And Bullet was true to his name!"

"What?" rang out from several quarters of the table. "What do you mean?"

"Only that with his ears laid back and the bit in his teeth, he streaked straight across the Park with no regard for bench or bush, tree or pond, horse or carriage,' deviating neither to the right hand nor to the left,' as

Scripture says, and on into the sunset. Did you ever hear from him again, Georgiana? No? Well," he looked lazily at Bastien, "that goes to show you, does it not?"

"What does it show, Monsieur Brougham?" the Comte asked in a tight voice, for no one had vouchsafed an answer and Brougham's gaze remained upon him, his brows still raised in expectation.

"That a man should never try to fight above his weight, especially if he must be led to the challenge and, more so, if it is to impress a woman. Are you familiar with the saying, *Monsieur le Comte*? From the sport of boxing."

"*Oui*, I am familiar with boxing, Monsieur Brougham," he answered, his eyes ablaze and his jaw so flexed with indignation that he could barely speak. "I have been in the ring."

"Do tell!" Dy crooked a disbelieving brow. "Perhaps you might indulge us with your tale when the ladies are not present, *n'est-ce pas*?" He sat back in his seat and waited, careless for the Comte's response.

À votre plaisir, Monsieur. At your pleasure."

~~~&~~~

The tension in the dining room after the ladies had withdrawn was so marked that Darcy determined to end the masculine ritual as soon as it was decently possible. After creating the latent hostility that fairly radiated from the Comte, Brougham blithely ignored what he had wrought. Instead, it seemed his purpose to recall when he and Darcy were friends and rivals at university and his many visits to Pemberley during that time.

Bingley was fascinated by their stories, aware that he was being admitted into a past world that explained his friend in more depth than years of being his brother-in-law ever could. He counted it a miracle and a privilege that, without reserve, they welcomed him in.

Unconsciously, their circle of three tightened, leaving the Comte conspicuously on the verge and at the limits of his hold on civility. The whack of his brandy glass as he forcefully brought it down upon the dining table, recalled Darcy to his earlier decision.

"Your pardon, Bastien," he apologized. "Old friends, old times, you understand."

"*Certainement.*" The Comte's brief nod underscored his discontent. "So old, *Monsieur*, that you have much to talk about, *n'est-ce pas?*"

Darcy shot a glance at Dy, whose head was down in a study of his shoes, but the upturned corners of a smile were still visible to him.

"Come, let us join the ladies," Darcy drew them to the door.

When they had traversed the hall and the drawing room doors were opened to them, a wail of impressive strength and duration met their entrance. Its unexpected tone rooted them to the floor.

"Your heir, I assume?" Dy asked, coming up behind him. "Should you, ah ... *do* something?"

Shaking off his surprise, Darcy strode into the room to Elizabeth, whose rocking and attempts at soothing had not, it appeared, been at all satisfactory. She glanced up at her husband with a look of defeat.

"We have all tried to comfort him, but to no avail," she explained. "I was just going to take him back up to the nursery." Darcy reached for him.

"He is past reason, Darcy, I doubt—

"Let me try," he whispered, and lifted the infant up and to his shoulder.

"Here, you had better have a cloth," Georgiana advised and tucked one over her brother's shoulder and under the baby's cheek.

Brougham sidled over to her. "Does he do this often, your brother, Georgiana?"

She gave a little laugh. "I can only suspect; he seems to handle Alexander with wonderful assurance." They stood together and watched Darcy circle the room, patting the infant's tiny back, humming as he went.

"I am all astonishment," he honestly confessed.

Bastien approached them as they continued to observe Darcy's attempts to relieve his son's distress and asked Georgiana if she would not prefer to sit. He indicated a chair with an unclaimed companion nearby.

"Not just yet, thank you, Monsieur."

"Quelque rafraîchissement? Let me procure something for you."

"You are very kind; perhaps later." She smiled up at him, but it was perfunctory. Undeterred, he remained next to them for a few minutes then, with little grace, turned sharply and retreated to a chair near Jane and attempted to engage her in conversation.

Georgiana sighed beside him, causing Dy to look down into her face. He had no need to guess, he knew her so well. She was troubled and he was certain of the cause. "Can I help you?" he inquired softly. "You have but to ask."

"I do not know."

Dy noted that she did not say *what* she did not know. His mind flew about, touching upon the possibilities. *Uncertainty in general or particular? Had the young devil wheedled a pledge from her or,* his jaw clenched, *compromised her in some fashion, real or imagined, as his uncle had suggested?* He kept his eyes on Darcy, fearing that if they wandered to the Comte, he would betray himself.

"What I *do* know," Georgiana suddenly continued, "is that I am very glad you are here."

"Oh?" was all that he could respond. It was a good, all-purpose response, rife with the potential for further revelation. Few would suspect how well its simplicity served him or its higher degree of efficacy in delicate situations than any other. This time, however, it caught in his throat for fear of what she might yet say.

"I have been distracted of late, and your arrival has ... well, I find that I have missed you, my lord." How had she not known this when now it was clearly before her eyes?

Missed me ... missed me? His senses trilled a hopeful warning where, by all rights, there should have been none.

"I am in need of a knight, you see." She groped for the right words. "One with a sword ... and a heart."

Staggered by such a forthright admission, Brougham adopted a light touch. "You've dragons that need slaying, I take it?"

She laughed quietly. "In a manner of speaking. A stalwart friend ... no, more than that, a *compagnon du cœur*," She paused, then confided, " think you are very good at dragon slaying, my lord."

Lost for words, for perhaps the first time in his adult life, Brougham cast about him for how he should respond. What should he say? The next sounds he uttered had in them such formidable power that they might make or break his future. He must be to the point, yet allow that he may be misinterpreting the extent of her meaning. Carefully, he responded in kind.

"I am *very* good in that regard," he murmured, then added clearly, "and my heart is ever your companion."

The young woman beside him sighed again, closing her eyes this time, and a smile played about her lips. Although they had not touched, he could feel gentle strands of serenity enveloping her as she stood at ease beside him. He was still not entirely sure what their exchange had meant to her, but he was now utterly certain of his purpose.

~~~&~~~

After Darcy had proved his aptitude for soothing infants to an incredulous audience, the ladies, pleading country hours, bade the gentleman good night. The evening had closed with the men withdrawing into an alcove to entertain themselves with cards. The points were set at a modest rate, wine and spirits lay close by, and the servants had supplied a plate of sandwiches to sustain their play.

All was present for a convivial end to the day. Darcy took his friend aside and imparted a wish that he would resist the temptation to further needle the Comte that night. "I wish him to Jericho as soon as may be, but for now, he is castaway here and we must suffer him until it is possible for him to leave or Georgiana can be persuaded to give him up."

"Pray God, it is as easy as an open road to be relieved of him *and* his uncle," Dy replied. At Darcy's shocked exclamation, he recollected that he had not told him of the uncle. "Yes, shockingly enough! The driver is actually his uncle, le Baron de Neuville, the younger brother of the Comte's mother. He is here to ensure that the Comte carries through. Ugly fellow!"

"How so? I've not actually seen him."

"As a young man, younger than the Comte is now, he was caught by Danton's *Ministère* and tortured. He still bears the scars. As a result, he is also a very dangerous man, totally devoted to the Fronsac family and its return to power. He will be of more concern when the Comte informs him of his failure in securing your sister."

"His failure?" Darcy asked him sharply. "You are sure? He has had her in his pocket! How –

A soft grin played across Dy's features. "I am absolutely sure. There is no question in my mind. He has lost her."

"Dy," Darcy replied grimly, "you must understand: after Elizabeth and Alexander, she is the most important person in my life! You assure me, unequivocally, that she is safe from them?"

"Darcy, Darcy!" he spoke in a hushed voice. "Nothing is certain save God's will! But to the very best of my ability and with the help of your people here at Pemberley, we *shall* be rid of them, hopefully without bloodshed, very soon."

"Bloodshed?"

Dy put a warning finger to his lips. They returned to the card table. Later, Dy swore that he had not put the Comte in considerable debt to him by design. It was just that "the man was a d-mn poor player" and further, he could not be blamed that Darcy's beast had distracted the Comte by coming in the card room and growling at the man's every move.

Chapter 17

Sunday, December 19, 1813

Early Sunday morning stable boys were sent off to gather news of the condition of the road to Lambton and report back whether Pemberley's folk would be able to attend services. It was the Fourth Sunday of Advent, the last before Christmas itself. Everyone at Pemberley, from master to scullery maid, would be greatly disappointed if they could not.

By seven o'clock, the boys were back, red-faced and grinning with happy news. The road was passable by sleigh all the way to the village and, even now, teams were tamping down the snow. Wheeled traffic might expect to make it to church without difficulty.

Giving them each tuppence for their efforts, Darcy watched from the portico steps as the boys skipped and shouted out to the world that the road was clear and Christmas had arrived in Lambton. Chuckling, he recalled that twenty years ago, he had been sent out with the stable lads by his father on the very same errand. He re-entered the house to meet Reynolds, who awaited the news. "Very good, sir. The staff shall be apprised. A light breakfast, as is the custom then?"

Darcy nodded. "As is the custom." He returned upstairs to the start of a flurry of activity. Elizabeth was just finishing with Alexander when he entered their bedchamber and she looked over at him with a beatific smile. "Alexander has been wonderful this morning, letting his mama sleep so late! Good boy!" she tickled his chin. Annie Fletcher's knock recalled them and upon Elizabeth's call to enter, Darcy retreated to his dressing room.

Because it was Fourth Sunday, Elizabeth and Jane would join them for breakfast instead of taking it in their rooms, so Darcy and Bingley waited in the hall for them to appear and walk down together. Down the hall and around the corner, they could hear the sound of Georgiana's door opening and her light step approaching.

She came to the juncture of the two halls and stopped, her attention on something in the other direction. Darcy caught his breath. Was it the dress? Her upswept hair, curled so cunningly? Was it her poise? The look of expectation upon her face? He could not decide, but there was no doubt: she was the picture of their mother, so lovely that she had been the most sought-after young woman of her Season, so unaffected that she deigned to choose their father, an untitled gentleman and neighbour, rather than the noblemen who had fallen at her feet. For a moment, he disbelieved that she was his sister.

Georgiana smiled shyly and Darcy watched as she held out her hand. Suddenly, Brougham appeared from the other hall and with the greatest delicacy possessed her hand and brought it around his arm. He looked splendid as well, even if it was in borrowed plumes.

Had he forgotten his pledge? Dy had never broken a promise to him but Darcy could only conclude that he had. *Two years, he had promised, and it had been only one!*

"Good L-rd, Darcy," Bingley exclaimed in a low voice. "Don't they look marvellous together? I never noticed."

Elizabeth and then Jane entered the hall and turned to see what their husbands gaped at. "Oh, my!" the two of them cried together and could only stare at the couple coming toward them.

Dy brought them both to a halt. "Oh dear, has the kitchen burnt down?" he inquired innocently of Darcy. "Or do we breakfast in the hall on Fourth Sundays?"

"No to both," Darcy answered tersely. "Shall we go down?"

Georgiana paled at her brother's abrupt manner and looked to Brougham. With a smile and a slight shake of his head, he patted her hand and escorted her after them.

When they were seated in the breakfast room, the pleasure of having their wives at the table and then the expectations of how the church would look that morning were discussed as they awaited Bastien. Minutes passed.

"Did you have a *very* late night?" Elizabeth inquired.

"Not *very* late, no," Bingley answered her. "He may, ah ... may have had a bit more to drink than has been his wont." He looked to Darcy and Brougham to further enlighten the ladies, but neither obliged him.

Finally, the door opened and admitted the Comte. With an uneven gait, he made his way to an open chair and sat down heavily.

"Good morning, Bastien," Darcy greeted him evenly, ignoring the evidence of imbibing that had certainly continued past the break-up of their card game. "We shall be leaving for services in an hour. Do you come with us?"

"*Non, non*, my family are good Catholics. Do you have a priest in your village?"

Catholic? How had that not occurred to him? Before Darcy could apologize, Bastien continued, "*Peu importe.* It does not matter; I have not been to Confession since..." He seemed to be trying to remember how long it had been, but then gave up. "So, you will all go to Lambton today?"

"Only for church," Elizabeth gently informed him. "Tomorrow, we prepare for St. Thomas's Day, which is on Tuesday this year. We will be busy here and in Lambton all day. Darcy's aunt and uncle will arrive then and spend the holidays with us until Twelfth Night."

"Yes, Darcy has told me," Bastien fiddled with his toast.

"Have you heard from your father, Bastien?" Jane asked solicitously. "He must be worried about you."

"No, *Madame*, I have not. Perhaps a message will come today. The roads are said to be open, but to York? *Je ne sais pas.*"

"How would your father know where to send it?" Bingley thought out loud, then coloured. "Pardon me! Not my business."

"I think Grayson has sent to my father through channels."

"Channels?" Dy repeated.

Bastien's eyes flew open and his lips compressed into a line. "Channels? *Excusez-moi*, I meant that he sent through a courier. My English," he shrugged his shoulders.

... is quite good. Dy regarded him silently. He had heard him speak with the best of English accents in the stable work room where he had not been at a loss for the right words. *It is his French that is lacking, peppering his speech, as he does, with the most common of sayings, though his accent is excellent. Reveals a good deal about his past.*

Darcy rose from the table. "It is time we prepared to leave. Bastien, while we are gone, please avail yourself of a mount from the stables, the books in my library or whatever you might fancy from the kitchen. Just ring any bell and although the staff will be smaller this morning, someone will be with you directly."

"*Merci*," he responded, and though he followed them out the breakfast room door, he did not mount the stairs but stood there looking after them. Darcy cast Dy a questioning look, as they ascended. Dy only shook his head, but when they had reached the top and the Comte had disappeared, he put a hand on Darcy's sleeve.

"I will not be long; take care for your sister and I will catch you up by horseback," he whispered and reversed course, hurrying back down after him.

There was no time for disguises, hardly time for a warm coat in which to follow the Comte out of the house and to the stable's work room. He was in search of his uncle, of that Dy had no doubt. The Comte had seen that he had lost to him in his pursuit of Georgiana. He most likely had gone with the bad news to his uncle the night before, hence the inebriation still in evidence this morning. If that was so, de Neuville might have put into play another plan, as he had hinted. He was not a man to give up on such a prize after only one attempt at it and he had already revealed his alternative—kidnap!

Dy steeled himself and entered the work area from a side door, creeping silently toward the sound of voices in the room that had served them before. A flood of angry French assaulted him as de Neuville dressed down his nephew. Evidently, he had hoped that the boy had retrieved his standing with Georgiana somehow and he lashed out in disappointment that he had "failed yet again."

"I followed your instructions to the letter, Uncle, so it is your fault, not mine!"

"*Parler en français,*" he roared, "*Combien de fois dois-je vous le dire?*" How many times must I tell you?

"I cannot even *think* in French if you will shout at me! How many times have I told you *that!*"

"*Bah! Idiot!*" de Neuville walked away from him and slammed the table with his fist. He closed his eyes and took a deep breath, continuing in French. "This is the result of your father's stupid decision to send you to England as a child! You are more English than French!" He paused a moment to nurse the decade-old quarrel he had lost with his sister's husband.

"No matter," he continued, "it is arranged. A coach will meet us in the village tomorrow just as it is dark. In all the celebration of the St. Thomas day, you will bring the girl and we will take her to a cottage I have found, do you understand? There must be no question that she must make a marriage with you. We have a priest." He took Bastien by the shoulders and held him in an iron grip. "*Est-ce que tu comprends?* Do you understand, Bastien? Your family must not have suffered so long for nothing!"

Brougham slipped out of the work room, and quickly traversing the courtyard, he entered the stable before he allowed himself to feel the smallest particle of the white-hot anger welling in his chest. Even then, he forced it down, knowing from long experience that indulging in any emotions now would only cloud his judgement and, if needs be, his aim, should it come to that. He hurried back to the end of the stable where the horse that had so valiantly brought him to Pemberley was still in a stall. His saddle still lay straddling one of the boards and his saddle bags hung from the hook where he'd placed them.

Opening one, he reached inside and brought out the box in which his Richards pistols were housed and proceeded to load them both, carefully loading the flint into the cock and measuring the black powder before tamping it down in the muzzle. The ball in a patch came next and everything was tamped down again with the ramrod. He put the small bag of primer into his waistcoat pocket and, shoving a pistol in each pocket of his coat, retraced his steps to the work room.

<center>~~~&~~~</center>

At the conclusion of the Advent service, Darcy and Georgiana searched for Dy among their fellow parishioners but it was soon evident that he was not there, that in fact, he had never arrived.

"Why would he not have come, Fitzwilliam?"

"We won't know until we return home, Sweetling," he replied, trying his best to sound unconcerned. He helped her into the sleigh and tucked the robe around her, then did the same for Elizabeth.

"He never came, did he?" she murmured to him.

"No, he did not. We must get back as quickly as possible." He then added with more honesty than he'd offered his sister, "I'm worried."

The trip back to Pemberley was a quieter one. In his anxiety, Darcy jumped from the sleigh before it came to a stop in the courtyard, and ran up the portico stairs and into the hall. Reynolds met him there, his face stern.

"Lord Brougham requests you meet him in the book room, sir."

"He is well?" Darcy gasped for breath.

"Well? He is quite well, sir, as are we all," he replied. "But only you should go to the book room, sir. No one else." He bent towards Darcy. "His express orders, sir."

Eyes narrowed, Darcy turned and strode down the hall.

"Ah, Miss Georgiana, Mrs. Darcy, welcome home!" Reynolds signalled the footmen to begin helping them with their coats and wraps. "Mr. Bingley and Mrs. Bingley, welcome."

Reynolds's strange effusiveness put both Georgiana and Elizabeth on their guard. "What is it, Reynolds? What is wrong?" Elizabeth asked quietly while Jane and Charles were divested of their coats.

"I'm taking Jane up to rest," Bingley called over his shoulder as he assisted his wife up the stairs. "Enjoyed the service, but she's wearied to bits."

"Reynolds will send up some hot chocolate, won't you Reynolds?" she pinned him with an arch look.

"Yes, ma'am."

In unspoken accord, they waited for the pair to reach the upper hall, then she rounded on him. "Reynolds?" she ground out.

"Nothing, ma'am. We have had an exciting morning here, to be sure, but nothing is ... ah, wrong."

Elizabeth's face took on a highly suspicious cast but before she could question him further, Georgiana broke in with her own. "Have you seen Lord Brougham?" Her voice trembled. "He did not arrive at church as he intended."

"No, Miss, I am to tell you that he was unavoidably detained and will see you after he has spoken to Mr. Darcy ... ah, in the book room," he began to repeat himself, "where he will admit only Mr. Darcy at present." Then, with a pronounced clearing of his throat, he abandoned his role as co-conspirator for his accustomed one. "Should you like some chocolate, Ma'am, Miss? In the Yellow Salon, perhaps?"

~~~&~~~

Striding quickly down the hall, Darcy grabbed the door handle, turned it, pushed, and immediately stilled. Dy sat before him at his desk, deadly-looking pistols in hand pointed across the room. Darcy peered around the door. The Comte and his driver, or rather, Baron de Neuville, sat there against his ledger shelf, tied to chairs and gagged.

On seeing Darcy, Bastien strained against his bonds and tried to cry out. Darcy looked back to his old friend. "What the devil, Dy?"

Chapter 18

Friday, December 24, 1813

"You can imagine my astonishment—or perhaps you cannot; for I was speechless—to find Brougham, sitting at the book room desk, pistols at the ready, aimed directly at the Comte and the Baron, who were gagged and trussed in chairs against the opposite wall!" Darcy paused to enjoy his aunt and uncle's reaction to his tale.

Lady Matlock gasped and looked across the dining table at Brougham in disbelief. "How ever did you manage it, Brougham?" In her experience, Darcy's friend had always served as little more than an entertaining decoration, unsuited to any exertion beyond recovering a lady's fallen glove.

Brougham shrugged. "I had brought my pistols but had forgotten them in my saddlebags. Once I surprised them, the stable lads came to my call and, brawny lads that they are, overpowered the two and bound them up."

"But to bring them in the house, into Darcy's book room?" she persisted.

"It was cold, ma'am!" Dy shivered. "Surely, you would not wish me to remain in the stable!"

Lord Matlock snorted at Brougham's delicacy. "So, you are just an hour ago returned from a whirlwind trip to London. Turned over these miscreants, did you?"

"Yes, my lord. Darcy was kind enough to lend me those same lads until we were safely in Town."

"And then what? I do not understand why you—"

"A deposition was required, Matlock, and only I could supply it," he explained with a self-deprecating smile, "and also, I knew someone who knew someone who knew what do to with such creatures, which simplified the entire matter, you see."

"Well," Lord Matlock shook his head. "Quite an adventure! My son Richard should have been here to help you. Over in Spain, you know. We are indebted to you, Brougham, keeping our girl here safe from such despicable scoundrels!"

"I shudder to think," Lady Matlock added and then proceeded to do so.

Darcy rose from the table and the remains of a memorable Christmas Eve dinner to invite them all to repair to the drawing room. Slowed by their partaking of the splendid feast, they rose to their feet. Darcy stood at the door as they filed out and crossed the hall. Dy, who was the last in line, stopped at the door and putting a hand on Darcy's arm detained him until the family could no longer be seen.

"A word, Darcy?" Dy murmured.

"Now? Can it wait—"

"No, I think it cannot. We both will be on pins and needles all evening."

Darcy sighed unhappily. "Then come to the book room where we can speak in private." They walked to the room in an awkward silence, and in silence they remained until Darcy had closed the door and turned to face Dy, his arms folded over his chest.

Dy lighted a candle at the desk and standing ramrod straight before his friend, he then honoured him with a bow. "I've come to ask your permission to make my address, Darcy, and to ask for your blessing."

"You promised me *two years*, Dy," Darcy's voice was hard, "and it has been only one!"

"I know," he responded quietly. "I had fully intended to bide by our agreement under the situation as it stood then."

"As it stood then?" Darcy queried. "A pledge is a pledge, Dy."

Brougham regarded him steadily. "Yes, it is," he admitted, "but consider this: she has since had her Season. It was brilliant, but she has returned from it unattached. Has she spoken a name?"

Darcy's lips twisted.

"No, she has not," Dy answered his own question, "because there is no one she has favoured until the Comte du Pont-Courlay arrived at your door."

Darcy winced.

"Although, the Comte's intentions were tied to intrigue, his reason for them is held quite commonly among our own class." He held out his hand, "You know this, Darcy! Why else have you asked me to watch over her since Wickham?"

Darcy went cold. "You know about Wickham?"

Dy shook his head wearily. "Of course, I know. *How* is neither here nor there, but this is: I love Georgiana and have known it for well over a year. I have kept my pledge against the hope that she would return it naturally and of her own accord after gaining experience in our wider world."

He took a deep breath. "I have good reason to believe that my hope has become reality and my address will be accepted. If you wish, I will agree to another year, but only as her acknowledged betrothed."

He stepped away to the window to give his friend a moment to absorb his terms and looked out upon the clear, star-filled night. The silence between them was awful. From his stance at the window, he spoke into the night.

"Darcy, my friend, I cannot be forever fighting off other men who desire her for her fortune! Let it be settled, and allow me to protect her as my beloved wife."

He heard Darcy stir behind him.

"Your work for His Majesty?" Darcy asked.

Dy turned about. "Finished! I will resign as soon as I return to London. It may take a little time to be accepted."

More silence. Dy watched in doubtful hope as a variety of emotions rose and washed over his friend's countenance. Suddenly, Darcy advanced upon him, his hand out. Clasping Dy's, his close on it was firm.

"You have my unreserved permission, Dyfed Brougham, and the grateful blessing of all my family. I know you will love and care for her better than any man I know." Truly, Darcy knew he could ask for no better man on whom to bestow her hand than the one before him. "There will be some surprise among the family, I warn you! If they only could know all that you have done!"

Dy closed his eyes, only a small smile communicating his immense inner joy. Opening them, he responded to Darcy's words with a snort of laughter.

"Well, they cannot! Their 'surprise' upon learning the truth about me would be more than I could possibly bear. Let them think what they think, Darcy. I'll win them over. Wait and see!"

~~~&~~~

Georgiana could not but notice that Lord Brougham and her brother had not joined them in the drawing room. The traditional fare of Christmas Eve was beautifully laid out upon various tables amid the glowing candles and holly-graced decorations reserved for the season. Her uncle, Lord Matlock, wove back and forth from the tables to the hearth, impatient for a piece of Christmas cake and a glass of Darcy's exceptional brandy. Aunt Matlock was happily wedged between Elizabeth and Jane on the divan, cooing over little Alexander, who had just been delivered to his mama for that very purpose.

Hearing steps, she looked to the door, but discovered only her brother, checked at the entrance. He looked about the room, and when he had found her, cocked his head and motioned her over. She went to him quickly, a question upon her face.

"Where is Lord Brougham?" she whispered. "He has not left us!"

"Not at all," he murmured back and, taking her hand, looked deeply into her face, knowing that after this night, she would never be the same.

"Lord Brougham asks that you go to him. He is in the library, Sweetling."

Georgiana went still, her hand trembling in his. She nodded her understanding. Darcy released her hand and turning from her, stepped into the drawing room and the bosom of his family.

"Darcy, where have you been?" his uncle bellowed jovially. "Beginning to fear you had forgotten the cake! Not a proper Christmas without cake!"

~~~&~~~

Georgiana tread lightly down the halls to the library, whose door lay open in invitation. A fire had been lighted at the hearth, for she could see its flames dancing in reflection on the polished marble floor. She paused to listen. All was quiet. Only the crackle of the hearth flames laying hold of seasoned wood broke the silence. She looked about her at the empty hall. Was Lord Brougham truly within or had her brother been mistaken?

There was a loud snap as fire met sap and she jumped, startled for a fanciful moment into perceiving the dark hall and library as the lair of a dangerous, secretive beast.

The sound of a man clearing his throat came from within the room and quickly dispelled her impression. Laughing to herself at her silliness, she took a deep breath and stepped inside.

Lord Brougham stood at the hearth, his arms crossed and his back to the young flames. The flickers of light playing about his face disclosed a countenance of such uncommon solemnity that she slowed and then stopped, uncertain what she should do. "My lord?" she breathed out softly and then wondered whether it was even possible that he had heard her.

Realizing that his earnest regard had confused her, Dy dropped his arms and allowed himself the slightest of smiles, a smile which, had he known it, was rather like a crooked grin.

"Georgiana, my dear," he began. "I was afraid that you might not come."

"Afraid?" That he could be afraid of her was a revelation. Emboldened, she looked at him in playful doubt. "I cannot imagine such a thing! You are my sworn knight, are you not, my lord?"

"Your *compagnon du cœur* was the term, I believe, a companion of the heart." He looked into her eyes as if in search of something, waiting for something, but his own heart was too full to keep his peace any longer.

"Have I slain your dragons, Georgiana?"

Georgiana nodded, smiling shyly. "Yes, my lord, all of them."

"Do you think that your heart could be companion to mine, advanced in age as it is?" His question was serious, but the smile that he had been hard pressed to hide in his desire to honour this august moment threatened to burst from him.

His uncertainty astonished her. "It is even now in your possession, my lord. Can you not feel it?"

In only a few strides he was before her.

"Georgiana ... my love," he began. Possessing himself of her hand, he dropped to his knee. "Would you do this devoted knight the *very* great honour..."

Epilogue

The announcement in the papers of the engagement of Miss Georgiana Darcy to His Lordship, Dyfed Brougham, Earl of Westmarch, occasioned every bit as much gossip and astonishment as the bride's brother had predicted. Lord and Lady Matlock were the first to learn and were frank about their doubts, but Brougham soon cajoled them into guarded acceptance of the match. When he had encouraged them to note how happy was his bride-to-be and the rank to which their marriage would raise her, they began to smile tightly and nod. But the *coup de grâce* that secured their enthusiasm was handily delivered when Darcy, upon Brougham's prompting, requested that Lady Matlock's knowledge and taste be consulted on every aspect of the wedding and with no expense to be spared.

Lady Catherine de Bourgh knew nothing of the Earl of Westmarch save that in her day his late father had been known as a sad wastrel. It was her considered opinion, she wrote, that the current earl was likely to be one as well, bad blood being what it is. She predicted that her niece would certainly rue the day she entertained his suit and called upon the shade of her late sister, Lady Anne, to convince Georgiana to abandon her folly before it was too late. It should be noted that in a postscript, an acceptance of the invitation to the wedding for herself and Anne was enclosed.

The *Ton* was almost astonished into silence, if that can be imagined. That the fool and fribble they had known for years and who had decorated their parties with his wit and wiles had managed to secure the most celebrated debutante of the Season and one of the wealthiest girls in England was not to be comprehended! Their curiosity abounded and would last for the better part of a year after the April wedding that all agreed was the *do* of the Season, surviving even the abdication of Napoleon.

The London wedding of Miss Darcy and Lord Brougham was a grand affair, enhanced by the attendance of His Royal Highness and his particular friends as well as officials from the Home Office. As to why they should have come, no one knew and attributed it to a quirk of His Highness's or a fondness for Brougham's sharp cleverness when it wasn't directed at himself.

Lord and Lady Westmarch (for Brougham thought it time to assume the title) merely smiled and thanked one and all, but especially her ladyship's brother Fitzwilliam Darcy and his wife Elizabeth. The firm friendship between the new brothers-in-law and the love between Georgiana and Elizabeth were remarked upon even by the most cynical of Society's principal critics. "All well and good," they said among themselves as the Westmarches departed on their wedding trip, "but what would come of it all?"

A Christmas Carol

So, now is come our joyfulst feast;
Let every man be jolly;
Each room with ivy leaves is drest,
And every post with holly.
Though some churls at our mirth repine,
Round your foreheads garlands twine;
Drown sorrow in a cup of wine,
And let us all be merry.
Now, all our neighbours' chimnies smoke,
And Christmas blocks are burning;
Their ovens they with bak'd meats choke,
And all their spits are turning.
Without the door let sorrow lye;
And if for cold it hap to die,
We'll bury't in a Christmas pie,
And ever more be merry.

—George Wither, 1622

More from Pamela Aidan

Thanks so much for reading my work!

If you enjoyed *A Proper Darcy Christmas,* an honest review at Amazon is very welcome.

The more reviews an independently-published book receives, the easier it is for new readers to discover.

For news of my new releases, follow me on my Amazon author page, Facebook, and blog: TraipsingAfterJane.wordpress.com

PREVIOUSLY PUBLISHED WORKS

Fitzwilliam Darcy Gentleman series

An Assembly Such as This

Duty and Desire

These Three Remain

NOVELLAS

Young Master Darcy series
A Lesson in Honour:
A Pride and Prejudice Christmas Story

SHORT STORIES
The Riding Habit
Jane Austen Made Me Do It

What's Coming Next

*Don't' you think that
It is time attention was turned to
Colonel Richard Fitzwilliam?*

June 1815: Colonel Richard Fitzwilliam and his cavalry unit are called from the Duchess of Richmond's lavish ballroom to the muddy fields of Waterloo to meet Napoleon's reconstituted host intent on retaking his empire.

Wellington prevails, but things go horribly awry for many British troops at the Battle of Waterloo. In days a letter arrives at Matlock Hall with the dire news that

Colonel Fitzwilliam is among the many missing in action. With no meaningful evidence of a search for the lost, his family is extremely alarmed! Who can find Richard in the post-battle chaos of Belgium? Lord and Lady Matlock turn to their niece's new husband Lord Dyfed Brougham, the Early of Westmarch and former agent for his Majesty for help. But before Brougham can even embark, a second letter arrives at Matlock Hall. Colonel Richard Fitzwilliam is charged with treason!

Charlotte Collins is in desperate straits. The Reverend Mr. Collins has passed on to his reward by way of a dining mishap, leaving her with no home of her own and an incorrigible two-year-old son. A few months with the boy in their home has worn his Lucas grandparents to the bone and although young Collins is heir to Longbourn, its current owner remains quite healthy. Where can Charlotte, with young William in tow, go to find refuge and a little peace? Pemberley, perhaps?

Love and Honour
A Pride and Prejudice Romance

About the Author

Pamela Aidan has lived all over the U.S. but has found her heart's home in the beautiful Pacific Northwest with her husband and mischievous Australian Shepherd, Sassy.

A Proper Darcy Christmas comes after a twelve-year hiatus filled with the directorship of a new public library and teaching literature to middle and high school home schoolers.

Visit me online on Facebook and at
TraipsingAfterJane.wordpress.com
I'd love to meet you!

Made in United States
Troutdale, OR
12/19/2023